Crushed Ice

Crushed Ice

Eric Pete

www.urbanbooks.net

Urban Books, LLC
78 East Industry Court
Deer Park, NY 11729

ISBN 13: 978-1-60162-380-5
ISBN 10: 1-60162-380-1

First Mass Market Printing March 2013
First Trade Printing February 2010
Printed in the United States of America

10 9 8 7 6 5 4 3 2 1

Distributed by Kensington Publishing Corp.
Submit Wholesale Orders to:
Kensington Publishing Corp.
C/O Penguin Group (USA) Inc.
Attention: Order Processing
405 Murray Hill Parkway
East Rutherford, NJ 07073-2316
Phone: 1-800-526-0275
Fax: 1-800-227-9604

Dedication

To all the dreamers,
Those who hear the voices,
Those who see the unseen and what could be,
And those who dare to make it happen.

Acknowledgments

Guess who's back? Yep, another year as a son, husband, father, and author. As I write this, it feels like I'm getting that second wind in life. Feeling better now than I have the previous two years combined. Not what I expected, but what is life if not unpredictable, always surprising and astounding us with its ability to provide both great joy and incredible turmoil. The only thing certain is that life will go on, with or without you. That makes your choices and how you relate to others so important during your "limited engagement" on this planet. Do you get on the bus, or watch it roll by? Which pill . . . the red one or the blue one? But enough random observations. Let's get on with the program.

This novel that you hold in your hands weaves in and out of the many worlds of my past novels, glancing off a few things you might find familiar, while still charting its own wild course. (Dare you to identify all the past characters and their novels. E-mail me once you've read it. I'll tell you if you're right.) I guess its roots formed when I wondered about the back-story of an incident that occurred in *Lady Sings the Cruels*. While you may have seen the handiwork of my newest creation back then (and maybe in one other story), this is where you meet him face-to-face.

Poor you.

Then again, *maybe you don't meet him*. He can be elusive, after all. *smirk*

I'd like to thank my family, Bee-bee, da Baby, Mom, Dad, Virginia, for loving me, warts and all. Know that I love you unconditionally too. Mom, thanks for never discouraging my love of books or those old black and white movies with which I grew up.

To my agent, Portia Cannon: Thanks for being so caring and accessible. To Lisa Cross and Cross The Network: Thanks for all you do behind the scenes. To the team at Urban (Carl, Martha, Brenda, Natalie, Kevin) and Kensington: Thanks for allowing and encouraging my growth as an author. Thanks to the art department for the awesome cover!

My dear friends and infamous ghost readers this go-round—Shontea, Jamie, and my fellow author, Jacqueline: Thanks for always being there and taking the time out of your life to let me share this certified straitjacket of a story with you.

A special thanks goes out to Elda Cantu, Max Lallemand, and Amy Paine, my friends of many skills and dialects. I appreciate you putting up with my odd requests and strange phrases in need of refining as I wrote this story, even if not all of them made it onto the final pages. One day, I can only hope to be a fraction of the linguistic masters that all of you are.

Thanks to the reviewers, interviewers, and media who've shown my stories love: RAW-SISTAZ, Urban Reviews, APOOO, Book Remarks, Gail Norris, Ella Curry, Nakea Murray, Adai Lamar of KJLH, Hal Clark of 98.5 WYLD, Erik Tee and Gina Cook of 107 JAMZ, Angela Jenkins of KBMS, Mista Madd of 97.9 The Box, Michael Baisden, Glenn Townes, Dedan Tolbert, and Jake McDonald.

To the readers and book clubs who've been with me from the beginning or who've only recently picked up my works: I thank you for coming back for more. A special shout-out goes to everyone, friends old and new, who I met during my *Sticks and Stones* and *Reality Check* tours. Thanks for making them so memorable and monumental. From the bookstore signings to the book club meetings to the National Book

Club Conference, it meant a lot seeing you out there on the road.

To my fellow authors: Dwayne, Kim, Victor, Mary, Gloria, Nancy, Lolita, JL, VeeJay, Kendra, Reshonda, Electa, Pat, Donna, Lissa, Earl, Shelia, Tracie, Jessica, and all the rest who are out there in the world, trying to provide an escape, bring some joy to someone, or teach important life lessons through the tales we tell, may you all be blessed with continued success. I'm honored to know you and have you in my life.

In closing, I'll go old school on ya, back to my Lake Charles days, and simply say, *The Adventure Continues*. (Some of you will get that reference. LOL)

Any omissions were completely intentional. Yep. I hate you that much. J/K.

NOW READ THE DAMN BOOK!

Can't stop. Won't stop. Believe that.
Eric

From out of the sun, I make out an old farm truck as it meanders along. It's the only thing I see on the road ahead. I pray it's not a mirage.

Maybe I'll make it.

Then I hear its steps.

Pads under its paws, gliding over the rock and sand as it closes on me. Tap. Tap. Tap.

No wonder they stopped shooting.

"Fuck!" I curse, knowing I shouldn't be wasting a single breath. I push harder as more of the truck comes into sight. It's an aged Ford. Paint long gone.

I could almost cry.

I begin waving my arms hysterically to get the driver's attention.

I step into a tiny crevice, abruptly jamming my knee. I almost go down, but somehow balance myself with one hand. Stumbling, I resume my frantic pace. A vulture is circling overhead, just waiting on me to fuck up. He'd get leftovers at the plate of Truth, though, for my four-legged pursuer would get dibs.

Now I hear it panting. Imagine it leaping into the air, its teeth intent on finding my throat and not letting go.

My tortured feet touch scorching pavement as the truck swerves to miss me. As it passes, I grab the railing, yanking myself from my dire

Chapter 1

Now, like a mutha

I bleed.

I sweat.

I hurt, running as hard as I can while barefoot. Not an easy feat.

Feat. Feet.

Only a warped mind can find humor in the midst of disaster.

My feet burn as I push on. I can't tell whether it's from the hot ground or simply my pain.

They've stopped shooting. I realize that as I burst through the prickly brush. Feels like razors slashing across my calves.

A small country road looms ahead. As delirious as I am, I wonder if they're waiting for me.

It would be an easy way to end it.

I can't think that way.

My mind will save me.

It always does. It's all I have.

predicament while almost pulling my arm out of its socket.

The pit bull's head smacks into the tailgate just as I raise my legs to safety. That doesn't stop it, as it shakes it off and tries to leap again, its teeth bared.

The elderly Hispanic man begins to brake, looking to see what cargo he just picked up.

"Go! *Ir! Ir rapidamente!*" I yell.

Seeing the desperation in my eyes, he doesn't debate the issue.

As we speed off, the dog's masters arrive at the road as well, their black truck kicking up a plume of dust and rocks. Shooting but missing me and Grandpa. Rather than continue their pursuit of me and draw further attention to themselves, they hastily drive off in the opposite direction. I'm luckier than I deserve to be this time.

There will be reckoning, just not now.

"*Gracias, señor*," I mumble before passing out in the bed, the desert sun still beaming down on me.

Chapter 2

One month ago . . . Sin City/Las Vegas

Secluded, away from the pounding beat of the main stage, the supple bodies writhed across us in a sensual choreography of flesh. Satin and sex at our bidding. Quaking ass cheeks clapping beneath my very nose. Breasts grazing his pursed lips.

"What do you propose?" I asked, knowing the answer before he did.

"I want him to pay," the aging, yet still physically impressive athlete answered. He should be enjoying the pussy, the ultimate salve for his wounded ego; up in here instead. Of course, if he did that, he'd have no need for me. Peaches, one of the dancers here at The Standard, as in "gold standard" of gentlemen's clubs, had earned her finder's fee by putting him in touch with me. She was one of a loose network of people around the country, from barbers to A-list celebrities, who knew how to reach me when opportunities arose.

I fixed things. No, rather, I broke things. Manipulating and molding situations to suit my customers' needs. Felt regret . . . sometimes.

But not too often.

"You sure about this? People have done worse," I said.

"Worse? He's fucking my wife, man!" San Antonio Jackson, the future Hall of Famer and soon-to-be retired wide receiver for Oakland, snarled, jarring Peaches from the lap dance she was giving him. I motioned for her and her dead sexy co-worker to leave us alone in the VIP room. She stuck out her hand, and I placed a hundred dollar bill in it. There'd be more later. Once we were alone, I spoke again.

"No offense, but wasn't your wife a performer in a place like this when you met her?" I asked, anticipating him charging out of his seat just like he did. I was waving a red flag in front of this bull. He also stopped, as expected, without laying a hand on me. Always did my research. Even knew the man's stats from back in college. Leaving nothing to chance was a priority.

"Peaches told me you could help, but I'm not about let you insult me, bro. That was many years ago when my wife was a stripper. I have worked too long and too hard at my career and my life for this kind of betrayal."

"Does anyone else know? About the two of them being lovers?"

"They're not lovers. He barely knows her," San Antonio scoffed. He returned to his seat, probably besieged by images of his wife in the throes of passion at the hands or dick of a person thought to be his friend. "Nobody else knows about them."

"And you don't want anyone else to know. Especially your teammates."

"Precisely," he answered. He couldn't tolerate the slap to his manhood among his peers. "I took Andre under my wing when I came over from Cleveland. Kid was a rookie . . . fucking fifth round draft pick. Fifth. Showed him how to read defenses, how to get a step on his routes. Even how to dress and carry himself in public. Now he's a starter. And he's fucking my wife."

"What do you want me to do?"

"Ruin his life," San Antonio answered. "Take away what he thinks he has."

"Well, your money cleared."

"Damn straight," he remarked. "So you better deliver."

"I think it best to leave Andre's ruination in your hands."

I produced photos of Andre Martin, Oakland's new golden boy, looking less than golden. I placed them in San Antonio's hands, allowing him to digest what he was looking at.

"Are these real?"

"Does it matter?" I answered as I stood to take my leave. He broke from his examination of his new weapon of vengeance to look up. "They're not photoshopped. But do you really care?"

"Yes—I mean, no. What if he's . . ."

"Get tested. Both you and your wife. If you still care about her."

Funny how things work out. Andre Martin wasn't even my target when I'd snagged those photos last month. Just an extra fish in the net I'd cast on my last visit to Vegas. One person's misfortune had turned into another opportunity.

Peaches and her friend were working two customers by the bar as I exited from the back. The DJ was spinning some David Banner.

"Did I do good, baby?" the overly endowed girl from Georgia asked as I passed. As she turned, she rubbed those big things against me as she had with San Antonio.

"You certainly did," I replied with a kiss on the cheek and another nine hundred in her hand. "Keep up the good work."

"Ahem." The other one cleared her throat. Godiva, I think was the name she went by. "Anything for me?" she asked, more demand than request.

What I had for her wasn't money. She was sexier, more assertive than Peaches. Wanted to take her back to VIP and finish what she'd begun. But staying in one place too long can be dangerous. From out of my pocket, I fished five large and placed it in her hand. Peaches didn't like it, but competition between the two would do me good. And maybe I'd be back in town with time to spare one day.

By the time I emerged from The Standard, I'd already changed my clothes and ditched my faux accent. In Brooklyn, they thought I was from the Dirty South. In Chicago, they thought I was from London by way of Kingston. Out west, they thought I was an Ivy Leaguer. Here in Vegas, it depended on who I was dealing with. Like the high-dollar suit I now wore or the T-shirt and jeans I'd discarded, everything was an accessory.

As I drove away in my rental, I checked my rearview mirror, thinking my mother would have been proud.

For I am Proteus, wearer of many forms.

Chapter 3

Way Back . . .

"Now, you know what to do if somebody knocks, right?"

"Yeah, Mommy. Don't answer." I glanced at the multiple chains and locks on the door. Could barely reach the top one without a chair to stand on.

"That's my baby," she gushed. They called her Leila Marie, like Marie was her last name. She got rid of her last name when we made it to Hollywood. She called it Hollywood, but I don't think that's where we lived. Hollywood wasn't supposed to look like this.

"When can I go to school? I'm bored in here."

"What about the books I got from the library?" she replied.

"I like reading them, but I don't have any friends. I wanna play."

"You don't need friends, Truth. I'm your friend."

"But you be at work all the time. Then you come and leave again," I whined.

"I'm doing this for us, baby. You gotta network in this town," she admonished, putting on her makeup. "Mommy's gonna make a name for herself; then everything will be all right. Better than all right."

"When can I come by your work? I like that lady who plays like she's crazy."

"We'll see, li'l man. They don't like kids on set, but at least you get to see me on TV."

My mom told me of her dreams since coming here from New Mexico. I liked it better out there. At least I got to see her more often. As long as I could remember, she'd tell me stories of how she left New Orleans, pregnant with me, en route to her acting career in California. She didn't make it to California just then.

I stopped her.

Now that we were here, she made up for lost time.

"I don't like staying here by myself. Can we go back ta New Mexico? I miss playing with my friends."

"Now, you know we can't do that, baby. How am I gonna find a nice daddy for you if we go back? Speaking of that, did you see him yesterday?"

"Yes, ma'am." I sighed. My mom was seeing the guy who played Randall Fischer on *Promises for Tomorrow*. In addition to her soap opera, where she played a poor mother from across the tracks, she made me watch his. He didn't know about me. She said Hollywood needed to think she was single, so she could succeed. We barely went anywhere together these days.

I don't think anybody knew about me. Sometimes I would sneak outside onto the parking lot, where I would watch the people. I didn't quite understand all that I saw.

I told myself that one day I'd return to New Mexico, where everything was nice.

"How does Mommy look?"

"Beautiful," I replied as rehearsed.

"Good!" She kissed me on my forehead. "Behave yourself and maybe I'll bring you back a treat."

I followed her to the door and quickly closed it behind her before someone in the hallway saw me or tried to come in. The hallway smelled like pee-pee, so I usually held my breath.

I didn't feel like watching TV today. I turned back to my books on African and Greek mythology, escaping to another world. Kind of like my mom did with her acting.

Chapter 4

Months earlier . . . Dallas

I was running late and didn't want to miss her. I jogged up McKinney, dodging the antique trolley car that ran on the regular, while getting both facts and falsehoods straight in my head. My flight in to Love Field last night was rough, on top of losing my luggage. Luckily, I always kept the most important things close to me. Crossing Lemmon Avenue, I slowed to a casual stroll. No matter the attire, a black man running through trendy Uptown tended to attract unwanted attention.

The bookstore in the West Village shopping center is where we always met. Entering the front door, I surveyed the general vicinity. The line of cash registers to my right were half-staffed. More people were gathered amidst the rows of magazines on my left. The display in front of me told of an upcoming book signing by a local author. I laughed, thinking of a private joke. I tapped the bag at my side to ensure my laptop was inside and headed toward the smell of roasted coffee beans.

"Your usual?" the barista asked from behind the counter.

"You got it, man," I replied as he prepared my dose of Seattle's Best. In reality, I didn't care for the Vanilla Bean blend, but it wasn't for him to know. I plunked down my cash and took a sip from the oversized ceramic mug.

She sat in a comfortable chair nearby, situated midway between me and the magazine row endcaps. I watched her tend the cup whose blend mirrored mine. Brown curly strands cascaded around the perimeter of her noble face. Full, sensual lips indulged in the coffee, her mouth appreciating every detail of the warm brew. Minus one obvious change, she was as poised and elegant as the day I first saw her.

At first, I walked past her. Took a seat at a nearby table where I could place my laptop. Still close enough to speak to her. I watched her as her fingers moved over the pages of her book, dark sunglasses obscuring her eyes. James Patterson. Her favorite author.

Opening my laptop, I powered up and waited for my Internet link to establish. When ready, I sent a packet of information courtesy of my latest trip.

Before I could exit, the recipient replied, a window opening to her *thoughts*:

U r fast.

Told you I'd get it, I typed.

Okay to post?
What do you think?
This is good stuff. REAL GOOD. Remind me to kiss you—if I ever see u.
You won't see me. Just credit my account.
K. U know if u ever came forward, I could make u a STAR.
No thx. Like my life the way it is. Out.

"You changed your cologne," my friend said as she paused from her reading. I clicked, disconnecting my online connection with my associate, then shut it closed.

"You're scary," I replied. "Then how did you know it was me?"

"Your musk. I caught it when you tried to sneak by me."

"Excuse me?"

"Not like that." She smiled. I liked it when she smiled. "Your natural odor. It's pleasant. You've been running or something?"

"Maybe just a little." I walked over, giving Collette a hug. "Didn't want to miss seeing you today."

"Whatever," she scoffed. "Where've you been? Didn't *see* you last week," she joked as she turned her head toward the sound of my voice.

"Still coming with the stale jokes."

"Hey, you keep coming back."

"Had to meet with my editor," I lied.

"How is that story coming along, Hemingway?"

"So far so good."

"You ever going to read it to me?"

"Too early to tell. You know how I am about that. All my stuff is under a pen name. Maybe you've already read some of my stuff and didn't know it."

"So you really are James Patterson. Would you please autograph a Braille edition to one of your biggest fans?"

"You missed me," I teased, feeling unusually calm around her.

"I'd never admit it."

One year.

One year of this unusual, casual friendship. A somewhat weekly rendezvous of sharing over coffee. No names. No strings. No invitations to one another's places, in spite of my knowing where she lived. Thoughts in general and wisecracks were our sustenance in spite of the mask I wore. But what purpose is a mask to one that cannot see it?

"Another coffee, ma'am?" the barista asked, bringing over a fresh cup out of habit. On the small table beside her was an additional cup. Either she was hitting the caffeine hard, or Collette wasn't alone. I thought I knew everything about her.

Shame on me.

"What's wrong?" she asked, grasping my arm. I flinched, distracted as I was.

"Nothing," I replied, suddenly realizing how nice her hand felt. Was it just in response to someone intruding on our unique space?

"Your voice doesn't sound like nothing."

"Just remembered something I need to do," I stated calmly.

"Oh," she mumbled, tinged with regret. "I wanted you to meet someone. Sophia!" she called out.

From somewhere between the News Publications and Arts and Hobbies sections of the magazines emerged a refugee from the Fashion and Beauty section. In her hand, she carried a copy of *Essence*, featuring Beyoncé on the cover . . . again. Although casually dressed in tan shorts and a white blouse, her face was flawless. Her height, demeanor, and stride said, *I am model. Hate me, bitches.*

"Collette, this your friend?" she asked. Accent was southern California. Maybe Inglewood, although she tried disguising it as non-regional. Another person with a mask. Wondered what Collette had told her about me.

"Yeah. He's being shy. Was about to leave, but I wanted the two of you to meet." Collette rose. I reached out to help her, but she shooed my hands away. Independent, she was. Brought a smile to my face that I'm sure she could sense.

"Sophia, this is my friend . . ."

"Chris," I answered for her, referencing the name on my lease. I wrestled with my natural instincts to change accents, morph into something else before this stranger. "Pleased to meet you."

"That's messed up," Collette spurted. "This whole time, you won't give me a name, and as soon as you meet my cousin, you're volunteering everything."

"You mean you didn't know his name? Y'all are weird," Sophia said with a flip of her hair in mock disgust.

I laughed, not quite sure how to answer.

"He's an author, cuz. He likes his anonymity, so I play along."

"Oh. Anything I might know?"

"I refuse to answer that," I said with a wink at the beauty. Her deadly smile hinted at an interesting tale.

"A man with secrets can be sexy."

"See. That's why I wanted you to meet him, Sophia. Ain't he sexy?"

I'm not sure how Collette's admission struck me. Should I have been flattered that she thought that way about me? But if she did, how did I feel that she would prefer hooking up her cousin instead?

"I suppose so," Sophia coyly answered. "Want me to describe him? Or have you touched his face already?"

"Can't say that I have, but it's not like that."

"Y'all are boring. Chris, is it okay if my cousin touches your face? She usually does it when she first meets someone. Don't know why she didn't with you."

"No, I don't mind," I answered, every fiber of my being protesting to the contrary. Sophia had me off guard and I didn't like it. I should've left as soon as I saw the extra coffee cup.

Sophia took her cousin's hand, guiding her in close as I stood stationary. I now found my private space shared with not one, but two others. Sophia stood before us, one hand resting on each of our backs as she moved Collette closer toward me. My personal boundaries violated, the three of us could've shared a breath. Those tender yet sensitive fingers caressed my features, creating some sort of emotional circuit between the three of us, completed by Sophia.

Surprisingly, being exposed before Collette felt liberating. I closed my eyes, letting her touch flow down over my eyelids and across my nose. Her fingers stopped at my lips, making me nervous. She had to detect the slight tremble as I contemplated kissing the tips of her digits.

"Nice," she said with a smile as she removed them. "You are very handsome, *Chris*." Either the newness of my name hadn't set in, having probably imagined her own name for me long ago, or she didn't believe me.

"My cuz said you were about to go? Too bad," Sophia remarked. "We were going to get something to eat. Probably at Dragonfly at Hotel ZaZa. Collette's supposed to show me around."

"As you can tell, my cousin's about the finer things in life," Collette teased. "She's staying with me for a while, so you'll probably see her around the neighborhood. Maybe you can show her around some, since I have some limitations."

"Would you, Chris? I mean, I don't want to intrude on my cousin's turf with you, but . . ."

"I have to check my schedule, but I can let you know."

"Good. Want to take down my number? Or do you want to give it to me? Your number, that is."

"Careful. She's flirting with you," Collette joked. I think. The two of them were messing with my perceptions.

I took down Sophia's number, avoiding divulging mine. Probably wouldn't see her again if I was careful. Giving Collette a hug, I shook Sophia's hand then left them in the bookstore.

Back on the street, where I was free of their spell, my cell rang. The one I didn't want Collette's cousin knowing about. I glanced around, ensuring no one was listening, then answered.

"Yeah," I answered in a tone different than what I'd been using moments earlier.

"Truth, how are you?"

"Fine. What you want?"

"Is that any way to talk to me? After all I've done for you?" he asked. "Are you still in Dallas? Trying to repent, my boy?"

"What do you want?" I asked again, tiring of him already.

"I have a job for you. That is, if you're not too busy freelancing these days."

"Who told you I was freelancing?"

"Don't take me for a fool, my boy. I'd like to treat you to a show. Tomorrow. Call me when you arrive in town."

I snapped my phone shut on him, cursing that I wouldn't get a chance to enjoy some down time.

Chapter 5

It was a rainy night in Houston, but the bowels of the Toyota Center erupted with light and energy from the show being put on at its core. Not one to ever trust the man I was to meet, I walked past the concertgoers, only stopping to point to the occasional restroom for the impaired or to read someone's ticket to guide them to their seat assignments.

"All these fuckin' kids. They gonna make me pull out what little hair I have left," the middle-aged woman, adorned like me in red and black, muttered. She guarded the access to the Toyota Center suite level with as much enthusiasm as Fox News covering the President.

"Yeah, they like roaches," I mumbled with a dose of Fifth Ward swagger I'd picked up that she didn't question when I shuffled by.

He'd left a ticket for me at Will Call, but I preferred doing things my way. Coming upon his suite, I walked past his guards, entering like I'd done the previous three, as if to check on accommodations for the tenants.

The well-stocked suite overflowed with curvaceous women of all shades, along with a few of his newest music projects, evidenced by the expensive chains around their necks. All of them seemed more interested in networking than in the concert going on. Made it easy for me to slip past.

I found him seated in the box beyond the confines of the suite, watching the concert as the *U.S. Icon* winner and runners-up performed on their nationwide tour. The most talented of them, hailing from H-town, was celebrating a homecoming of sorts before her fans. The girl broke into a remake of an old Stevie Nicks song, "Edge of Seventeen," putting a more urban spin on the timeless rock classic.

Stroking his salt-and-pepper goatee, the older man in the sport coat eyed her as if she were prey. Odd, considering all on the stage below were already signed to others.

"You had me come all the way for this?" I asked, walking down the five short steps to meet him.

He looked at my attire, smiling as if amused. He couldn't like my sneaking up on him though.

"Hey!" he yelled into the suite above. "Everyone give us a moment."

The multiple conversations, from silicone versus saline to the best party at which to be seen, halted. Everyone shut up, wondering what record mogul Jason North would want with a Toyota Center employee.

"Now!" he screamed for emphasis, in case they refused to understand his first command. As everyone filed out into the hallway, his guards ran in to see what the fuss was about. One of them recognized me, infuriated that I'd walked in right under their very noses.

"Too late for running in here now," he rebuked them. "It's okay. Wait outside the door." We watched the three black-clad monsters exit. Knowing Jason, he'd probably have them fired and replaced by morning.

"Have a seat."

"I'd rather not. What's up?"

"You used to be a member of our family back in New Orleans. Now you just want to sulk and scowl? What kind of life is that anyway?"

"You know how it goes. You need something, you call me."

"Know that singer down there?"

"Duh," I replied. "Natalia. She won that *U.S. Icon* shit. She's not signed to you, so . . ."

"Don't presume to know what I want or what I need."

"Whatever."

"Do you really think that lowly of me? And what I do? You aren't one to talk, Truth."

"That's where you're wrong. I know what I've done and what I continue to do, so I really am one to talk. What do you need?"

"Information on Natalia. For future use."

"Real or created?"

"I'll leave it to you. Natalia has a friend that auditioned for me years ago. I like to prepare for future eventualities."

"And you think dirt on Natalia will make her help you with this friend? A basic blackmail play?"

"You're good. Hell, you're the best. You are a true artiste. That's why I tolerate your freelancing . . . and costumes like this."

"You tolerate my freelancing because you have no choice. I'm not your property, Jason. Remember that. The secrets I know include yours."

He glared, reflecting on events in pre-Katrina times, when someone else really ran things. Most in the On-Phire Records family suspected what I knew for a fact. If not for our unique relationship, Jason would probably have paid to put me down.

"Secrets are rarely a one-way street."

"Fuck you."

"Such disrespect. After all I did for you and your eccentric mother . . ."

"Don't talk about her. You have no right."

"But I do. She is my sister. And you won't even give me the respect I'm due, nephew?"

"If I thought you were due respect, like the rest of these fools, I would give it to you. Look, I didn't come here for a fucking family reunion. Are you going to let me do my job?"

"Of course," he relinquished. As he spoke, the audience erupted in applause. The beautiful and talented recipient of their adoration had gained my attention. Unfortunate for her.

"No one dies?"

"No. I know how squeamish you are from that prior mishap. Just get some dirt that I might be able to parlay into something more."

"And my money?"

"Double. I'd like it done quickly."

"What's next on her schedule?"

"Las Vegas. At least for the next couple of weeks. One of those music awards shows. Nice town for whatever vices someone may have."

"Viva Las Vegas."

Chapter 6

I wanted dearly to make that drive back up I-45 to Dallas and hit my bed, but I stuck around a little longer. Figured I'd get a head start on my latest job. A few well-placed calls and I found myself at the Gibraltar Lounge on Louisiana Street in Midtown. Right where I needed to be.

"Five hundred?" he asked, not sure he'd heard me correctly. Perhaps over the DJ's music he thought he'd misunderstood.

He hadn't.

"Yes," I replied.

"Just to get her attention?" He was still surveying the business card I'd handed him by the soft, intimate light of our surroundings.

"That's what I said."

"Is this some kind of reality show?"

"Exactly. You weren't supposed to know," I answered, deciding to go along with the idiot.

"Where are the cameras?"

"Everywhere. Even back at the hotel. If you're able to get her there."

"And if I get her back to the hotel with me, I get a thousand dollars?"

"You got it."

"How much do I get for tapping that ass?"

"Nothing from me. That's your bonus . . . if you're capable of it. But if you're going to spend all night talking to me instead of being on your game, then maybe I should find another contestant." I cringed at how my prodding manipulations sometimes reminded me of Jason. Although my own man, my time with him had rubbed off in nefarious ways.

"Nah, nah! I got this," Anthony, the part-time model and college student from TSU, boasted. Models were always useful tools. They were actors-in-waiting who stuck to the script, hungry for a taste of something better.

"Here's your five then. Don't forget: cameras are rolling, but we need you to act normal. Just do what you do and get the girl."

The boy took a deep breath, channeling his inner Clooney mixed with a dash of LL, before sauntering to the other side of the bar, where Natalia and her crew were celebrating the night's concert.

Didn't watch much of *U.S. Icon* during her season, but Natalia had grown before the whole country, from the childish country girl with the church voice into this chanteuse wrapped in a flowing gold gown. A massive brother impressive enough to be her bodyguard worked the fuck out of his touchscreen BlackBerry, oblivious to Anthony as he walked up, drink in hand. The tall, thin girl with wave after wave of curly black hair was the center of attention, so he was just another moth attracted to the light as far as they were concerned. His appearance made him look as if he belonged anyway—the reason I picked him for the mission.

One of Natalia's female friends didn't waste any time in stepping to him. Fine as fuck, I think she was a backup dancer, but not on his menu tonight. At least on my dollar. He looked at me, his pleading face wanting to know if this one would be acceptable for my fake scenario. I shook my head in the negative. It had to be Natalia.

Having more moves than I had given him credit for, he worked her friend into giving introductions. Natalia was cheery enough, welcoming him into their fold. But that was as far as it looked to be going.

"Whiskey sour," I ordered as I took mental notes about Natalia for later use. Anthony needed to try harder though. Another glance my way and I nodded, putting my own mad thoughts to the complex human equation as Anthony stayed in the good graces of his new friend, while working harder than a mofo to gain the attention of Natalia. Interesting that the other men in the group didn't indicate the slightest bit of competitiveness with the addition of another rooster in the henhouse. Some could be gay, but not all of them.

Anthony got Natalia's attention again, this time lacking subtlety. I couldn't make out what line he was feeding her, but it appeared to be compliments of some sort. Now Natalia's girlfriend was irked. She gave the rest of the group one of those *No, this nigga didn't just walk up in here and play me while trying to push up on my girl looks*. Only out of respect for the hierarchy did she sheathe her claws. Lucky for Anthony because his back was turned. When his hand slid against the small of her back, Natalia twirled out of his grasp. She'd either tired of his game, or noticed the disrespect being shown to her girl.

But my boy wanted that grand bad.

The cool, laid back vibe of the place was disrupted with the arrival of another entourage, greater in size than Natalia's. This group consisted only of men, filled with much swagger. Their leader wore a white wave cap atop his head, with a sleeveless blue hoodie and black warmup pants. I overheard one of the stragglers, recognizing the strong Haitian accent dipped in the syrup of south Florida. This wasn't their habitat. These dudes were grimy, street hungry. Pork 'n Beans Projects hungry.

"Anthony, meet Antnee," I muttered over my drink, sensing the ironic humor of the moment. On my iPhone, I did a quick Google search for info on the rapper, who had been seen recently in Natalia's company. Penny Antnee, the Miami rapper whose debut album, *Ain't No Small Change,* posted decent first week sales, was allegedly working on a duet for Natalia's album. Turns out he was a bit of a hothead who'd been in trouble with the law on more than one occasion. What rapper hadn't these days, when felony and misdemeanor could mean a difference of a hundred thousand units sold?

Bare arms weren't the code, for men at least, but Penny Antnee didn't care. He proudly displayed the tat on his toned right arm, pennies from heaven raining down from shoulder to wrist. On his album cover, those same pennies turned to dollars in his clenched fist. Cheesy, but none of my business. Poor Anthony was unaware of the bad neighborhood he was now in, until he was surrounded.

When "Penny" tapped him on the shoulder, he shrugged it off. When he did it again, Anthony told him to step off, as he was busy. In some crazy kind of way, the boy probably thought this was part of his challenge.

"Hell nah!" Penny yelled. I guess he and Natalia were working on more than a duet. His boys sprang into action, wrapping up Anthony before he could even string together a sentence. Natalia yelled for them to stop, but she didn't control them. They knew only one master and friend, and when he said to fuck Anthony up, that's what they proceeded to do.

The staff quickly intervened. Knowing they were outnumbered and not wanting their place destroyed, they urged Penny and his boys to settle any beef they had discreetly and off their premises.

As suddenly as they'd pounced, they just as quickly picked up Anthony and removed him for more of a talking outside. Fighting desperately to free himself every step of the way, he yelled to me for help. I ignored him, thinking ahead to how this might end. This wasn't Miami, so I figured throwing Anthony on his ass but sparing his life would win out. This was more about respect for Penny. It wasn't like Anthony had groped Natalia—just yet.

When most of his boys returned, they reported back to Penny. He was busy apologizing to Natalia and her people about their rudeness. The one I knew to be Haitian gave him a business card. Penny glanced at it then looked toward the bar where I was seated. Anthony's ability to talk that fast hadn't occurred to me. I think it was the lack of sleep on my part.

Oh well.

I surveyed what was going on around me, all the while bracing myself for the rapidly approaching storm. I glanced at the woman seated to my left, then at the bartender.

"This you?" Penny asked, the cascade of pennies down his arm ending at the fake business card I'd presented to Anthony. He dropped it on the bar beside my drink glass.

"Excuse me?

"This your card? Bitch-ass nigga said you gave this to him. Paid him money to disrespect Natalia. That true, boy?" His boys wanted it to be so true. It was my job to ruin the smiles on their faces.

"Sir, I don't even know who you are," I answered, choosing a disarming voice, but leaving enough bass to let them know I was a man nonetheless. The eyeglasses I wore didn't hurt either. "And I certainly don't have money to waste on

games. Now, whose business card is this supposed to be?"

The Haitian stepped up. "You pay that man?
You play games?" he asked.

"I'm trying to have a nice evening out with my
fiancée here. I don't know what that man told
you, but that's not my card. He'd been drinking
a lot before you came in. Now, I do know that
much."

I locked eyes with Penny Antnee a little longer than I preferred. My way was never to fix in
someone's memory, but to exist on the periph-
ery. But part of me said "Fuck it" this time. Like
I said, I was tired.

"She your fiancée?" he asked for confirmation.

"Yes," I answered, grabbing the woman's
hand as it rested on the bar beside me. I prayed
that she wouldn't flinch when I did so. "I don't
want any part of your mess. Can you just leave
us alone?"

"Yeah. Sorry about disturbing y'all," Penny
said, not wanting a PR nightmare with the "civilians" plastered on the front page of the papers.
The thug was transitioning to a businessman.

He and his boys backed off to gather up Natalia and her people. Other parties awaited.

"Excuse me," I called out.

"What?"

"Are you one of those rappers?"

He rolled his eyes before humoring me with a smirk and a nod of his head.

"Could I have your autograph? For my niece?"

After a few choice curse words, they walked away. No autograph for me.

"You are insane," whispered the raven-haired Latina whose hand I still held.

"You may be right."

I stayed around Gibraltar for another hour, making sure no surprises awaited me when I left. With the coast clear, I escorted my new friend to her car. The rain had stopped, but the parking lot was still slick. She clicked her remote, illuminating the interior of the ebony Corvette. Long, black, powerful, American. I knew of something else that matched her tastes.

"I think I owe this to you," I said as I fished her payment from my pocket. When I first arrived at Gibraltar, I'd offered her some money just to sit there looking cute and to go along with whatever I said. If I didn't need her, she'd still get the money.

"You don't have to pay me anything. I don't need the money. This was more excitement than I've had all year," the attractive middle-aged woman gushed. "And I just came out to escape my kids. Whooo! Wasn't expecting this." I didn't know her name and she didn't know mine. Kept things uncomplicated—and me safe.

"But that's how it works. I can't just expose you to that risk without giving you something. Now, please take the money."

"Maybe we can come up with something else to settle this. You're supposed to be my fiancé, right?" she teased.

I took a deep breath. "Married?" I asked.

"Yes," she said, revealing the dazzling ring.

"Happily?"

"He's a developer," she answered. Her eyes cut with disdain above her high cheekbones that I was noticing for the first time. "Spends more time staring at vacant land and blueprints than he does me."

"He's crazy. You're worth more than that," I said, the temptation evident as the danger from earlier subsided.

"Thank you. But a new shopping center in Pearland or The Woodlands is what gives him a hard-on."

"Maybe his shit doesn't work like it used to."

"Does yours?"

"Most definitely," I answered like the young stud she needed me to be. Wanted to taste her moist caverns, run my mouth across her golden hills, erect my own tower atop her plains, and drill to unknown depths until I hit a gusher.

"Then why are we talking about him when we should be fucking?"

"You don't even know my name."

"You would probably tell me a lie anyway."

"True," I said, discarding the fake eyeglasses I'd been wearing.

"*Sí, sí, sí,*" she chanted, her ass dancing wildly as I rode her doggy-style. On her knees, she engulfed my dick as if her pussy were insatiable. Be it inches or centimeters, she took it all, metric or conventional be damned, for neither could measure the depths of her hunger.

Hotel Derek is what I'd suggested, having a room already set aside for Anthony's challenge. Instead, she took me to a home in The Heights. Not her home though. One of their extra properties they had on the market. Fully furnished. Too nice a bed to be stared at by potential buyers.

The ceiling fan overhead clipped the streetlight cutting through the blinds, granting us an eerie audience of shadows on the walls. Her black dress and sandals lay in a hastily formed heap in the doorway.

"Um . . . harder," she begged. "Shit, you're making me cum."

Her nails clawed at the sheets as if trying to escape my grasp. I brought my hands over hers, intertwining our fingers. My pelvis smacked against her ass as I pushed harder into that luscious, creamy center. She thrust her full, round hips back into me, another orgasm claiming her as she took me on a magical ride.

"Does he fuck you like this?" I whispered in her ear, my hips working around and around. I corkscrewed in and out until she lay on her stomach, her feet dangling off the bed.

"No! No! No!" she screamed emphatically, tears streaming down her face as our bodies moved in rhythm. Her legs bent, feet curled up toward me like a yoga master. She braced her arms underneath, pushing herself up and arching her back to form an almost perfect "C" beneath me. Her sexual prime being fulfilled was almost a religious experience. "Please, please don't stop," she pleaded, for fear of losing the revelation of which she was in the midst.

Iris.

Her name was Iris. She felt the need to share that with me as I'd peeled her dress off her—before I'd kissed down her trembling, naturally tanned body and plunged my face into her damp, steamy pussy.

She wanted to give more of herself to me than I was willing to accept. What we were doing tonight was instinctual, no thought. Thought takes up too much of my life. Sex is the only time when my thoughts aren't necessary.

"I . . . I want you to cum," she growled as she sent another wave of warmth cascading over my swollen dick. Her sweat-covered body shuddered, losing all control and coordination beneath me.

Pounding harder and deeper into Iris, I appreciated the rare gift she'd given me. I felt it emerging from deep within me; tried to fight it.

"*Sí,*" she hissed. "Do it. Give it to me. *Damelo.*"

My ass cheeks tightened and my eyes rolled back as it roared to be free. I was no longer its master as my body gave in to Iris's plea.

I gasped as I erupted; my seed released and joined with her flow.

The choice bed dampened by our encounter, Iris purred beneath me, blissful dreams taking hold after a good fucking. To think she was just escaping her kids and a mundane life for the night. In her, I'd found an escape of my own.

"*Gracias,*" I mumbled, succumbing to the exhaustion of the moment myself.

The sun was still dormant when we emerged from the townhome.

"Feel like some breakfast? You must be hungry," she said. The wrinkles in her dress were visible as she staggered down the driveway to her car. I'd parked the 650i convertible on the street, so as not to block her in.

"Starving, but I have places to be. Stayed way too long."

"Guilty as charged," she said as she looked back at me. "If you ever need a place to stay or anything . . ."

"And I'd be tempted, too, but . . ." She could've been useful, but I guess I still had a heart somewhere in there.

"I know. You do crazy shit for apparently no reason. Not healthy."

I walked her to her car; gave her a tight goodbye hug, "Get back to your kids before they wake up. Maybe you can work off any remaining frustrations on hubby."

"I doubt it," she replied as I closed her door. She started the Corvette, a throaty growl emanating from its exhaust. She wanted me to kiss her. I couldn't. "But if he's able, I'll give it a try."

"That's the spirit."

"*Aparte del sexo, yo se que llevas algo bueno adentro de ti*," she intoned, figuring I understood. Aside from the sex, there was some good in me.

"You're just saying that because you still have that 'glow,'" I joked, rather than acknowledge such delusions.

"Try not to get yourself killed, okay?"

"Good-bye, Iris."

"*Adios* . . . whatever your name is," she said with a wink.

With a shriek of its tires, Iris gunned the auto down Hartman Street and zoomed around the corner, leaving me alone in the pre-dawn hours and dreading the long drive back to Dallas.

Chapter 7

I took a sip of the black currant iced tea, engaged in another conversation across the ether.

Anything new for me? Slow news day for these other busters. Need something major. Keep these hits up on the website, y'know?

Busy working on a job. If something comes up, I'll holler.

Please do. The bigger, the better. You know nobody's $$$$ is betta than mines. Where are you living these days?

Nowhere. Everywhere.

You know I'ma keep hounding you until we meet one day.

How do you know we've haven't met?

I typed, feeling silly.

U like fuckin' with a sista.

Smiling at her comment, I checked my receipt, waiting for my order to be called. Number 332—a side salad and a cup of the black bean soup. A light lunch was what I needed after all the drinking and whatnot in Houston. Had been eating too heavy recently anyway. Being swift in mind, as well as body, often went together.

The soup took me back to New Mexico. Reminded me of Mary's comfort food while my mother worked long hours at the inn where we stayed. Mary, who worked a different shift, was like a second mother to me. When we moved to California, there was no more Mary. And the comfort, as well as the food, was gone.

I opened a window on my laptop. Began planning for Vegas. I needed a flight and somewhere to stay. With a click from my wireless mouse, I opened another window, viewing dates of the music awards simultaneously. My mind began assembling what I would need and who to reach out to. Natalia, Natalia. Time to get to know you even better.

From inside Café Express, I paused from my multi-tasking to gaze across the street at the Gables Uptown Tower, on alert for faces, both familiar and unfamiliar, that might want to pay me a visit. A palace compared to the places I'd grown up, it was where I'd been living since moving to Dallas. Just one of many structures that provided me shelter, except this location had a different purpose from the others.

"Three thirty-one."

I glanced at my receipt again. There was a woman at the counter. Tall sister. Long brown hair with honey streaks that matched her jogging attire. Instead of picking up the order that had just been called, she spoke with the manager. She had an attractive stance, swaying rhythmically while she conversed. Perhaps a nervous habit, but it was inviting; drew you in to whatever she was saying. I recognized the manager, as I'd been here often enough to chill and unwind. He drove a red Nissan Versa with a dent in its bumper right next to the worn RON PAUL FOR PRESIDENT sticker. Grad student at SMU if I wasn't mistaken. And I rarely was.

"Three thirty-two," they called out over the loudspeaker. About damn time.

My laptop could stay open while I retrieved my lunch, but I was sure to log off from my conversation. The dirt that I funneled anonymously to the Internet gossip site 4Shizzle worked both ways. It was a nice side gig, courtesy of the information I gathered in my usual pursuits, but it also served my purposes as another tool in my arsenal.

"Chris?" the woman speaking with the manager asked as I walked by them. Not my name; I didn't answer.

"Chris," she called out again. This time, I looked in her face instead of admiring her body.

Fuck me.

Sophia. Collette's cousin.

The odds of her running into me were . . .

As I reached for my tray of food, I eyed the few other customers in Café Express and then the parking lot before turning my gaze back to my apartment building across McKinney Avenue.

Nothing out of place.

"Everything okay with your order, sir?" the man asked, sensing my hesitation. I just nodded.

I knew how this would have gone—if I'd set it up. Eye-catching beautiful girl, chance encounter . . .

Except it was Collette who introduced us.

And I trusted her.

The only person I trusted.

"Hey . . ." I replied, having put my fears to rest. Paranoia and guilt sometimes threatened to consume me. Collette stayed nearby, so it wouldn't be that odd that I'd run into her cousin. "I'm sorry. I forgot your name."

"Sophia," she said. Seemed like she was genuinely hurt by my feigned ignorance. "You eating?"

"Looks like it," I answered, being a smart aleck to break the ice. "What you up to?"

"Doing some jogging. Have to keep this body tight," she answered, drawing my eyes to the flat stomach that showed below her sport top. Sweat had begun to dry by her belly button. "Stopped here to see if they were hiring."

"Dressed like that?" I asked.

"Do you object? Hey, I was in the neighborhood. Not having any luck anywhere else," she huffed. The way she pouted her lips was amusing. Attractive on some level too.

"I'm surprised. I'd hire you. I mean, if I had a job to offer."

"You don't even know what I do."

"Besides modeling?"

"Damn. How'd you know?" she asked, a smile returning after the disappointment she'd shown over her name. "You're good. Either that or you're just trying to flatter me in hopes of getting into my pants."

"If I was doing that, it wouldn't take much," I teased, looking at the loose drawstring dangling from her waistband. "You want some lunch? My soup is getting cold."

"What's up with you and my cousin?" Sophia asked, having taken me up on my offer.

"Nothing. Collette's a good friend. Why? She said something different?"

"No. She doesn't talk a lot about you." Sophia devoured the remaining roasted turkey sandwich, leaving the sweet potato fries for last. For someone as thin as she was, putting away food wasn't a problem. Probably had the metabolism of a jackrabbit. Probably fucked like one too, but I digress.

"Should I be hurt?" I asked as I powered down my laptop. Wasn't going to get any work done with her in my presence, but this conversation was allowing me to figure her out.

"Not if there's nothing going on. What you writing about today?"

"About a guy and a girl. They're in a restaurant, and the girl asks too many questions."

"Hmph. Thought you were writing about Las Vegas."

"Why?" I asked, pretending I was unfazed by the curveball she just threw.

"Saw you had the Strip pulled up on your laptop. When you set your lunch on the table," she said matter-of-factly. "Vegas can be a wild place . . . if you know where to look and aren't afraid. Research?"

"Yeah, just a little research. How was your food?"

"Good. Thank you for paying for it. Remind me to return the favor once gainfully employed."

"What kind of work are you looking for?" I asked, curious and wanting to take control again.

"Anything," she replied. "Been on an interview every day. At first, they're all interested, and then . . . It's just hard. . . ." She trailed off.

"You have a record or something?"

"No."

"'Cause if you do, I wouldn't hold it against you. For real." With the people I dealt with, it was easy to empathize.

"Some legal issues back home. Collette doesn't know about that. She hasn't seen—*oops*. I mean, we haven't kept in touch over the years," she shared, cautious in her answer. "I'm just frustrated with things. Cuz is nice enough to let me stay with her, but with no job and no money, I'm going to have to move on."

"Back home?" I probed. "Cali?"

Sophia glared at me. "Yes. How did you know? I know Collette hasn't spoken with you since Borders. First you know I used to do modeling, now this. You're scary."

"Nothing to it. From your height and the way you carry yourself, I guessed at the model stuff. I've been around enough of them," I admitted. "I picked up on the Cali accent you try to hide. Just observant."

"Are you from Cali, Chris?"

"Been there. Been a lot of places."

"Never a straight answer from you. Like an eel," she said, snaking her hand through the air in front of my face. "Are you really even an author? Or are you trying to take advantage of my cousin because she's blind and loves books?"

"You don't know your cousin then. Just because she's blind doesn't make her dumb. She would tell you herself that I have been a perfect gentleman from the day we met. How is that taking advantage of her?"

"I dunno. Perhaps I'm just being overprotective. Chris isn't your real name though, is it?"

"Before I share all my secrets with you, you have to be willing to share all yours, Sophia."

"Fair enough," she relented as she dipped a sweet potato fry in some ketchup. "Is there anyone you know that can get me a job? Please. I need some real money to get back on my feet."

"Collette doesn't know anyone?" I asked, not wanting to get all caught up in her issues.

"Like I said, she doesn't know about some things. I'm used to a certain standard. Like it is around here," she said, happening to point directly at my building. "Bet you stay in one of these."

I didn't acknowledge her guess. "I'm a private person, and don't like people forcing their way into my life."

"That's not what I mean to do. It's just that running into you today is a sign. I believe in signs, Chris. I'm desperate."

"I have some work that's taking me out of town. Can't promise anything, but I'll see what I can do. I'll call you when I get back."

She leaned over the table, exposing the tops of her large Bs/small Cs as she came closer. I wanted to reach under her top and caress them, taste her sweat from between them. She closed her eyes, kissing me on the lips while I remained motionless in my chair.

"Thank you," she offered, no evidence of regret present in the low, trembling whisper that escaped her lips. "I'm willing to do anything."

Only a fool is willing to do anything.

But is a greater fool one who accepts such an offer?

Chapter 8

"Is that Kanye? Get his picture! Get his picture! Heeeeey, Kanye!" the shorter of the two glammed-out women yelled. They abandoned the slots they'd been playing, bumping me and several other passengers out of the way as we disembarked our American Airlines flight from DFW.

McCarran was brisk today with all the traffic arriving in anticipation of the music awards. As that day got closer, things would only get more intense. Downstairs, I grabbed my luggage then exited to hail a cab, ignoring all the limousine drivers picking up their VIPs.

At the curb, I only had to flash my watch while hailing to get one to stop.

"Are you in the music industry?" the bearded Turk asked as he checked his rearview mirror before pulling away.

"No."

"With the television network?"

"No," I said, adjusting the tie I wore. "Just in town for some meetings."

"Bad time for meetings, my friend. Music awards in town. No work. All party."

"Is that why all *these people* are around?" I asked, ensuring he would detect the false level of Ivy-league, buppie disdain I was projecting.

"Yes, yes," he commented. "Rock stars, rappers, groupies. Lots of groupies. You'd be surprised at what I've seen them do. In this cab even."

I grimaced, realizing my hand was resting on the seat where some of what he was describing probably occurred. I hoped he disinfected on the regular.

"What hotel are you at?"

"The Westin Casuarina. Somewhere quiet, off the Strip, where I can think," I joked. "By the way, where are most of the music folk staying? Want to make sure I steer clear if I want to hit the slots or something."

"Most of them are at the MGM Grand, where the event is taking place. Some want to be seen in that new hotel, Stratus. Beautiful." He laughed, defiantly flicking his finished cigarette out the window. "If you need to do 'something,' I recommend The Standard, on the outskirts of town, my friend. Prime ass . . . if women are your thing," he said, catching himself.

"They are, my man. They certainly are. The women are hot, huh?" I prodded just to be silly. Most of the girls at The Standard, as well as the owner, knew me in one way or another.

"Incredible. I take many a fare out there. Trust me. A handsome black man such as yourself? You would be highly sought after for their attention. You like big titties, yes? Would make me leave my wife if she didn't have so many of my children. . . . I kid. My wife is a good one."

My fun over, I checked into my hotel and went into work mode. The information I needed, I could've gotten from Jason through his On-Phire connections. Not wanting him to take any credit or know exactly how I worked, I passed.

Natalia was discreet. After an hour of calls and e-mails, I was still at square one. Most of my contacts at the hotels had nothing definitive either. But I had other ways of finding her.

"Who dis?" the voice asked, with blaring car horns in the background. I could tell he was hustling as he spoke. Busy day at the valet station.

"Certainly not a bill collector," I said from the blocked number that failed to register on his cell phone.

"Ay, man. Didn't know it was you," he said, his voice relaxing. "What up?"

"You seen Penny Antnee?"

"Yeah. They rolled up last night. This the new joint on da strip. Er'body want to be here, but management wants a *diverse mix*. Said they don't want no hip-hop heaven. We had to turn niggas away when we hit our quota in here."

"Anyone else with him and his boys?"

"Uh . . . yeah," he replied as he entered another vehicle, the familiar door chime pinging. "That girl Natalia, if you believe that shit about them being a couple. She and her people didn't count toward our quota, on account she's more pop 'n shit."

Another car blared its horn. My valet informant cursed in Spanish.

"You gotta go?"

"Yeah. I get my usual, right?"

"You might have the chance to earn a bonus."

"For real?"

"Yeah. I'll call you back in a bit with what I need."

I took a look out the window of my room. Gazed north at the back side of the Venetian and in the distance, the Wynn. My objective now lay just beyond those two beauties.

I closed the curtain and opened my suitcase.

"Time to go to work," I mumbled as I had so many times before.

Chapter 9

Way Back . . .

"Trent! Nooo! Don't go!" she pleaded, her throat raw and ragged from all her crying. He pushed her off him, determined to escape our tiny apartment. I don't know why. It was nicer than where we used to live. Still not Hollywood, but nice enough to have company over.

It had come to this.

To my mom, he was Trent Massey. That wasn't even his birth name. He would always be Randall Fischer from *Promises for Tomorrow* to me. He'd just taken over a company and jumped from a burning building with a baby in his arms in just a single episode last week. Hated to admit it, but I kinda liked him now. He was smooth.

"Why didn't you tell me about him, Leila?" he screamed. Acted like I was an abomination. I knew that word. Had been reading a lot.

I had a name.

"I'm telling you now, Trent," my mom moaned. "Baby, please don't be like this. He's my son. We can make this work."

"Work?" Randall Fischer from *Promises for Tomorrow* taunted. "You've been keeping this boy a secret from me and expect this to work? We've been seeing each other this whole time and you didn't tell me you had a kid? What were you doing with him when you spent the night? Until you had me drive you over tonight, I didn't even know you stayed on this side of town, Leila. Good grief! We're supposed to be married!"

"We still can be, baby. He's my beautiful son. I . . . I didn't know how you'd react. I'll even introduce the two of you. Come here," she said, grasping his arm tightly. He resisted at first, almost to the door and his escape. He relented though and trudged over to me under her coaxing. Mom was beautiful, and most men did her bidding, including me.

"Trent, this is my son, Truth. Truth, this is . . . Mister Massey. He's going to be your—"

"Leila, no." He jerked his arm away, combing his fingers through the curly blond strands atop his head. His foot tapped repeatedly on the floor. "I can't do this. I like you a lot, but I can't do this. Really. This would be bad for my image. I'm sorry."

Randall Fischer from *Promises for Tomorrow* exited the scene, never to return. My mom, Lettie Hunter from *The Edge of Nowhere,* was never the same. Some will tell you she hadn't been the same for quite some time. She spent the rest of the week alone in her bedroom. When she came out, she pretended everything was okay.

But it wasn't.

She was written off her soap opera.

Chapter 10

C'mon. C'mon. Three diamonds. Three diamonds.

Two.

Shit.

"Would you like something to drink, sir?"

"Whiskey sour," I replied to the scantily clad hostess. The tiny butterfly wings affixed to her back were made of illuminated neon, casting an eerie blue glow on her bare shoulders as she fluttered away to fetch my watered down tranquilizer. Above us, acrobats flew on scarves of azure and purple tapestry, safe from the clink-clink-clink of electronic bandits and babysitters to the populace below. Giant papier-maché birds hovered on near-invisible wires, making people do a double take. I was in the midst of a contemporary blend of *Alice in Wonderland* and *Cirque Du Soleil*, wrapped up in homage to those that dared to reach toward the heavens.

Can't leave out the killer prime rib at the buffet either.

Dressed like a tourist, complete with shorts, New York Yankees jersey, and toothpick in my mouth, I played the quarter slots. Killing time and minding my own business. My vantage point put me as close as I could be to the lobby without seeming like I was casing the joint. In spite of Stratus's infant status as a casino and resort, its management was made up of veterans. Cyber eyes were everywhere, tracking and mapping faces and mannerisms. I was doing something similar, except with two targets in mind and minus the gadgets.

My little angel didn't return as quickly as I'd hoped. I figured she'd abandoned me for the big tippers at the dollar slots. Such betrayal.

Whatever.

I'd stayed in one place too long, so I quickly finished off my credits.

At the valet station in front, I waited patiently then provided my ticket to a certain attendant. When he returned with my economy rental car, I walked over, placing a tip in his hand. He paused when the surplus amount I'd given him registered.

"I said there'd be something extra," I reminded him from behind my Ray-Ban aviators.

"You?" he asked sheepishly, unimpressed by my attire and beer belly, courtesy of a well-placed hotel pillow.

"It ain't the tooth fairy, son," I replied, borrowing the same accent I'd used earlier on the phone. "I need you to find out what room they're staying in. And someone to do something for me."

"C'mon. I'll introduce you to my girl Eva on staff. She might be able to hook you up."

"No. I need you to be in charge of this. You don't want to share that bonus, do ya?"

"Tru dat, but—"

"Just get that done for me and I'll call you later."

My valet friend met me the next morning at the Barbary Coast near my hotel. I'd ordered breakfast, but there was way too much butter on my toast. My friend continued his yakking, trying to dictate his own terms, while I pretended to give a damn about his concerns.

"No cutting in the walls 'n shit, right? Just a camera and nothing else. They'll do some bad shit to me if somebody finds out. Straight off-the-books kind of shit."

"Just a camera or two. Nothing else," I commented, dabbing the extra yellow goo onto the plate.

"You from Harlem, ain't ya?" Francis Martin Quinones from Queens asked. Yeah, I'd done my research, down to back child support and all.

"You got me," I answered with as genuine a smile as I could muster.

"Yeah, I knew it," he crowed. "Got that old school, Uptown swagger. I ain't from here originally, dawg. I'm from da BX." Correction: Francis from Queens by way of the Bronx.

"No way, dawg!"

"Yeah. Straight up, homie! Let me guess. Penny been talkin' too much ya-yo about 'East coast time is ova.' Somebody from back home wanna check this Miami fool, huh?"

"I'm not at liberty to discuss that." I let my coy smile reaffirm whatever he believed.

"Yeah, we gonna do this. Fuck Penny Antnee," he crowed, feeling we were suddenly a team. "Shit's getting crucial, son. I'd almost do it for free. Almost."

"Natalia sharing the suite with him?" I asked, almost as an afterthought. "Don't want her getting in the way of shit that's going to be going down."

"Huh? No. She's on a completely different floor, homie. My girl on staff told me. Been to her suite. She and Penny leave together 'n shit, but when they come back to Stratus, they go their separate ways. Nigga probably don't want sand at the beach. Place gonna be knee deep in honeys come this weekend."

"Well, just in case, gonna need a camera in her suite. Gotta keep an eye . . . on Penny."

"Two rooms? Man."

"I'll send more funds your way. If we do this," I said, sure to include him before continuing, "then we need to do this right, dawg."

Francis the valet beamed in the affirmative. "Yeah, you my boy, no doubt."

In the booth, we gave each other a pound over the table. Wasn't sure what I was looking for, but I was certain the coming days would provide me with something for Jason.

The elderly waiter approached our celebratory meeting. "Is everything okay?" he asked.

"No," I replied. "There's too much butter on the toast."

"Yeah. All that cholesterol 'n shit. You trying to kill my boy?" Francis the valet from da BX chimed in.

Chapter 11

Nothing.

A day of watching monitors and still nothing. Antnee and Natalia weren't together like I expected. And Natalia spent most of her time shopping at Caesars Palace and signing autographs at the Fashion Show Mall across the street.

Nothing for me to distort or use.

My phone rang, interrupting me from my sulking. Jason probably.

"Hello."

"You ain't been by the shop in a minute," the barber from Minneapolis said. "Got somebody who needs something. They want to speak to you."

"What do they need?"

"Marital counseling," he joked.

"Counseling costs. Are they willing to pay my fee?"

"Looks like it. Some girl. My sister does her hair. Won the Hot Lotto. She doesn't want to share with her husband."

"Is he a bad man?" I asked. "Or just a victim?"

"I don't ask. Do you really need to know?"

"No." After I responded, my phone beeped. Another call coming in. Jason. He could wait. Needed to figure out what to say to him anyway.

"You want to talk to her now? She's right here."

"No. I'll see you at the shop. Then you can introduce us."

"When? She's kinda anxious."

"I don't like to be rushed. I'll be in touch."

"Okay. But she ain't gonna like it."

"Then she can get somebody else. I'll pass."

"Aww, c'mon, man. Chauntel—"

"Chauntel. You called her by her name."

"Yeah. So?"

"At first, she was 'some girl'. Now's she's Chauntel. You're sweatin' me over this. You never sweat stuff. You're fucking her."

"Uh . . . what's that gotta do with anything?"

"Complications. Personal shit that I like to avoid. Don't call me again."

"Wait! Wait!"

"Good-bye."

Aside from my laptop, the light from the TV illuminated my room. I had more than a passing interest in the story unfolding over the nation's airwaves.

SOAP SCUM was the title beamed across the banner of the cable news broadcast.

Cute.

Made me smile a little.

I listened intently to the Filipina reporter's words from outside the L.A. County courthouse.

"In a stunning set of developments, soap star Trent Massey has been charged with multiple counts of possessing child porn. L.A. County sheriff deputies were seen removing documents from his residence, as well his computer hard drives, this morning. This is in addition to his stunning appearance and arrest before the nation as part of a network television child predator sting.

"I don't think I've seen such a staggering and swift fall from grace. Trent Massey, as many of you know, won his second Daytime Emmy last year for his longtime role as Randall Fischer on the popular soap opera *Promises for Tomorrow*. We've attempted to reach his wife, Janie Thomas, the equally popular actress, but have received a 'no comment' and a wish for the family to be left alone during these trying times. Mister Massey, through his manager, maintains his innocence, so we'll just have to see how this all turns out. Back to you."

Even though he claimed to have shown up at the house of the supposed child by accident, the kiddie porn found on his computer sealed his fate. His claims of receiving an emergency call to go there wouldn't bear fruit. The cell phone he'd answered, although identical in appearance, wasn't his. No phone records to verify his story, as the deputies had thrown him face down on the lawn with cameras rolling. A chore switching it out, but successful, with the help from his unhappy wife, Janie.

Amazing what fate delivers to the patient. It took a year of false information being fed to her about her husband to make the gold digger unhappy enough to want out. That was where I conveniently came in. Now she had enough publicity as the poor unsuspecting wife to last the rest of her career.

This was probably my masterpiece.

And I didn't even get paid for it.

I changed the channel to some HBO and went back to watching the video feed of Penny Antnee and Natalia's rooms. Nothing in his, but he finally showed up alone at Natalia's. She had too much of a good girl image, courtesy of handlers, to do anything in public, but behind closed doors . . .

Penny sat on her bed, waiting patiently for Natalia to get dressed. She'd just exited the shower and was still wrapped in her towel. The camera view showed Natalia as she dropped the towel in front of Antnee, mixed drink in hand. I watched her nude body dance in front of him, imagining what music was going through her head. Should've had audio, but wasn't planning on wiring two rooms. Don't know if a sex tape was what Jason wanted, but that might be all I would get out of the church girl.

My cell rang again. Jason calling back. I answered this time. Penny hadn't made a move on her in the room. They were joking about something, by the way they were laughing.

"Are you there?" Jason asked.

"Yes. Working on it," I answered.

"How's it going?"

Rather than taking what was a pretty hot piece of ass and putting it to her on the bed, they exchanged high fives. Penny, alpha male to the Nth degree, demonstrated a different demeanor than what I'd observed over the past week. Soft. Unusual. "Nothing yet," I answered Jason as Natalia fetched something to wear from the closet and showed it to Penny.

"We arrive in two days for the awards. I don't want to leave empty handed. Get me something soon. Even if you have to improvise," he urged before ending the call. That meant making something up as long as it was convincing.

As Natalia dressed without a hint of action, I went right-brain in my approach.

I found a number on my other cell phone that I'd almost deleted, until that day at Café Express back in Dallas.

"Hello?" she answered.

I walked to my window and pulled back the curtain, revealing a million dazzling lights.

"You busy?" I asked calmly as I tapped my fingers on the cold glass.

Chapter 12

"Not at the moment," Sophia answered. "Didn't think I'd hear from you, Chris."

"Where's Collette?" I asked, partially regretting this call.

"She's in the next room. Want to talk to her?"

"No. I'll talk to her later."

Her voice lowered. "Want her to know I'm talking to you on the phone?"

"I'd prefer that she not. Does she know about our run-in at Café Express?"

"No," she replied. "And I'd prefer that she not."

"Still looking for work?"

"Of course. Why? You got something for me?" she asked, perking up.

"Research. I need help with my research."

"Me? I get to help you with your book? Okay. Need me to come over . . . wherever it is that you live? Or do you want to meet somewhere?"

"I'm not in Dallas. I'm in Vegas."

"You know the music awards are out there, right?"

"I hadn't noticed."

"Wish I was there."

"That's why I'm calling."

Wearing a sport coat and jeans, I waited for her to emerge down in baggage pickup. The same batch of limo drivers held their signs aloft. This close to the awards show, the names were more familiar—Lenny Kravitz, Kelly Rowland, Maxwell, Tim McGraw, Young Jeezy. One of them I'd done a job for in the past, although they'd never be able to identify me.

The particular lady I was looking for had that same strut as when she emerged from the magazines that day at Borders. She dressed as if she were one of the musical demi-gods descending upon Sin City. Hair pulled back into a single pony-tail, brown leather jacket, designer couture T-shirt, and a pair of fitted jeans. For someone in need of ends, she certainly didn't look desperate. It was that whole "model thing" that I preferred in my pawns.

But unlike my other pawns, I was actually here waiting on her, instead of simply dispatching a cab with instructions. Wheeling her carry-on bag behind her, she came directly to me. I stuck out my hand, prepared to thank her for dropping everything, whatever that was, and hopping on a plane at the drop of a dime.

From behind her designer sunglasses, Sophia grinned. Instead of taking my hand, she kissed me again. This time I relished partaking of her lips and lustful tongue, savoring the flavorful lip gloss she wore. No point in work without some enjoyment. As our intensity subsided, I backed off slightly.

"What was that for this time?"

"Thanking you again. For getting me out of there," she said, wiping our excess from the corner of my mouth. "I love Collette to death, but she can be a little boring."

"I don't equate being cerebral and intelligent with being boring."

"That's because you got the hots for her."

I frowned at her brashness and presumptuousness. She hadn't known me long enough.

"Hey, I'm just joking. Don't get all bent over it." Eyes of almond flashed at me, followed closely by that deadly smile.

I gave in, my smile returning in exchange as I took her bag. "Let's get you out of here," I said.

We hailed a cab, Sophia working better than an expensive watch ever could. The two of us piled in for the brief drive back to the hotel.

"What did you tell Collette?" I asked, uncomfortable with so many unwritten rules of mine being broken by my actions.

"That I had to run back to Cali to take care of something . . . check on a job," Sophia recited rather nonchalantly. She was more focused on the world outside the cab as we drove up Koval Lane, avoiding the congestion and confusion of The Strip. Made me wonder if I'd regret this sooner rather than later.

"That didn't sound convincing."

As suddenly as her focus had drifted, it was right back in the cab with us and on point. "I'm always convincing," she purred seductively as she squeezed my knee.

At the hotel, I presented Sophia with the key to her room.

"You're in four-oh-five."

"I'm not staying with you?"

"No. Trying to keep this professional."

"Trying? I thought you flew me out here to try to seduce me."

"You think too highly of yourself."

"Sometimes. That has been a weakness of mine."

"Any other weaknesses you'd care to share?"

"Men. Sometimes."

We looked at one another in the lobby. "The spa's really good. Feel free to get a massage or something on me." I left her with her bags, sticking to my guns. I heard the roll of her luggage wheels across the carpet then onto the marble floors as she followed me to the elevator.

"Why am I here, Chris?" she asked before I'd taken a few good steps inside the lift. I held the door for her then pushed the button to her floor.

"Because I need you to help me," I replied.

"Oh, yeah. This research you mentioned. Why are we at the Westin anyway? You couldn't get a room for me at the MGM Grand or Bellagio?" she asked, reminding me of Collette's remarks about her cousin's high-end tastes. In reality, I could've afforded a suite in any of the hotels this town had to offer. But I operated safe. Off the radar. I shone only by design—and when I chose to.

"What can I say? I'm an author on a budget." I sighed, watching the illuminated numbers on the plate above the door as we ascended.

"Bullshit. You're not an author."

"Have you ever met one?"

"No, but I've met plenty of schemers. What do you want from me, Chris?"

"You want it plain, Sophia?"

"I'd prefer."

"I need you to do what I say, without a bunch of questions, and I will pay you. Can you handle that?"

"I'm here," she taunted.

"That you are," I said as the doors opened on the fourth floor. "Meet me in the lobby once you get settled in. Then we'll get to work."

Chapter 13

"How did you know my size?" she said softly as we walked past the very valet attendant who'd assisted me. If he recognized me, he gave no indication. His thoughts were on all five-foot-eight of Sophia's body that lay barely concealed by the silk in which his eyes were burning a hole.

"You're a model. I guessed."

"You're lying. You must've been checking me out."

The way she wore her hair up was nice.

"Get over yourself," I grunted, not daring to admit she was right. The camera I'd placed in her room didn't hurt in "guessing" what would befit a sensual shape like hers.

She gave me a stiff jab with her elbow. I pretended to be annoyed.

"Do you like it?" I asked of the chic silver Donna Ricco bubble dress she wore as if made solely for her. The bow at the back of the strapless number gave the impression of a splendid gift waiting to be opened by the right person, if he were lucky. I guessed right with the size eight sandals.

"I love it," Sophia squealed, tightening her grip on my hand. Mere days ago, she was broke and desperate. For what I required, I hoped the desperation remained.

Along with throngs of arriving guests, gamblers, and simple partygoers such as us, Stratus welcomed all to its grand foyer. On time, an acrobat swooped just over our heads in a choreographed dance meant to impress and draw our attention to the domed atrium above. In the center of the ceiling was the see-through floor belonging to Stratus's signature night club, Soar.

Ooohs and *aah*s came from the uninitiated. From the eccentric and equally eclectic super producer SmithSonian, who was there to check in, came his typical, "No flying while intoxicated, honey!" to the acrobat as she returned on scarves on high to her overheard perch.

Penny Antnee and his entourage strode into the hotel on cue, worming through the crowd as if a colony of ants. As they sought out the elevators, a small girl, weaned on daily doses of MTV, snapped a blurry picture with her cell phone. She pouted over the poor results.

"Lemme see," I said to her. She looked up, perhaps wondering who this fresh-to-def brother might be, before handing her phone over. From my vantage point, I aimed the Kyocera and snapped a good one of Penny, catching that famous tat-covered limb too. Penny's Haitian buddy with the ill temper was with them. He looked me dead in the eye as he fumbled with his phone, but absent any recognition from that night back in Houston. Moving on from me, his eyes fixated on Sophia's legs, but ended at the dress that began just above her knees. The gift wasn't for him, whether he was naughty or nice. He resumed his cellular dilemma, continuing his brisk pace to catch up with his boys. Call it a hunch, but that one I had to be careful of. As they disappeared from view, I returned the camera phone to the little girl and patted her on her head. Her father thanked me for being so kind.

"What are we here to do? What's the mission?" Sophia asked, unfazed by the sight of Penny Antnee and other celebrities milling around us. I hadn't expected her focus to be so keen.

"No mission," I answered, gripping her soft hand. "I just want you to have some fun."

The lie out of the way, I led her to the elevators.

***

We made it inside just before the occupancy cutoff at Soar, Stratus's hallmark rooftop nightclub, famed for its panoramic view of the Las Vegas skyline, and the transparent floor located in the center of the club. Penny and his boys had joined Natalia and her party in VIP.

The DJ spun some Kaskade, Paul Oakenfold, Rihanna and Wisin y Yandel to get the joint moving. But it was the singles by the sexy UK duo Booty Luv that sent Natalia into an impressive lip-sync rendition in front of her friends. When the DJ realized Natalia was in the house, he quickly did an intro and put on her music to cheers from their group. During all the excitement, I led Sophia closer.

Just outside VIP, I talked up a pair of newlyweds from Nebraska, in the process learning that Omaha had more black people than I gave it credit for. To them, Sophia and I were a couple who drove in from California to taste the good life. Every few sentences, I would gawk at the excess. Over the music, Sophia couldn't tell what I was saying to them, but she knew I was full of shit. She stayed at my side, enjoying the drinks I was paying for and showing her appreciation by backing that thang into me on occasion when the beat or mood hit her.

It wasn't too long before she tired of my new friends and ran off with me. On the dance floor's edge, she pulled me closer and kissed me again. This one lasted longer than the others, but the timetable ticking in my head allowed me to retain some composure. Penny's boys had reached the DJ, coaxing him to play some of Penny's non-radio-friendly hits.

"I know we're not here for fun," she yelled in my ear over the music. "What's the deal? Tell me what you need me to do. I mean it."

I said nothing at first. "I need you in there," I admitted as my eyes led her to VIP.

"I knew that's why you were standing around there. No way in hell that boring-ass couple is as exciting as me," she remarked, dabbing a finger in her drink and sucking the sweet liquor from it. "Who? Natalia, or that rapper Pretty Anthony?"

"You know who they are?"

"Duh," she said, giving me the stupid-face. I hated when people did that.

"And his name is *Antnee*. Penny Antnee."

"Whatever. I'm not big on rap."

"Well, you're going to need to know his name."

"He's my mark? What do you need? His wallet? Credit cards? Get him back to his room and knock him out?" She seemed to revel in her knowledge of things most scandalous.

"Damn. You don't play," I said, marveling at her bluntness.

"I'm no virgin."

"I don't know what I need yet. Just get in there with them and see what you come up with."

"Those boys of his look rough. I'm not getting caught in a gang bang, no matter what you're paying me."

"I'm not interested in him. It's Natalia that I need stuff on."

"Oh?"

"Yes. But if you get both of them back to the suite, that's okay."

"I knew you were a freak, Chris. But that's okay," she said, placing a kiss on my cheek. "'Cause I am too."

She abandoned me. Began her methodic move toward the restricted area, where champagne had begun flowing by the buckets, compliments of the platinum-selling nominee for Artist of the Year worth far more than a penny.

On the outside railing, I took note of an overly intoxicated starlet vomiting as she prayed to distant Luxor at the other end of The Strip. Katelyn McMahon, eager for press of any kind. While she hurled, her socialite pseudo-friend was busy shoving her tongue down the throat of Katelyn's boyfriend while he felt her up. I discreetly took out my camera phone, trying to decide what embellishments I would add to the photo's story. Once back at the room, I was going to throw a bone to the online press for a nice fee, all at Katelyn's expense.

Over by VIP, Sophia had approached the two large club employees, defenders against anything or anyone lacking status. One look at her and she was allowed to enter the Promised Land with no hassles.

Champagne mists hovered in the air behind her, bottles erupting in sprays under pressure. Across the invisible line, she smiled at me, escaping the pull of my gravity so she could move into the orbit of musical giants.

I slyly nodded and smiled back, impressed, for I knew Sophia would exceed my expectations.

Chapter 14

Sophia ingratiated herself into the group like she'd known them forever. The amusing part was the quiet wrangling between Penny's boys for a shot at her. Two of them, I thought, were going to come to blows. Penny, after some soft words from Natalia, stepped up and took charge of the situation.

After shutting them down, Penny cleared a seat for Sophia by him and Natalia. No longer on the fringes of the party, they offered her a glass of champagne, and things continued popping as if nothing had occurred. When David Guetta's "Love Is Gone" came on, she and Natalia sprang up, wilding out together on the tiny table, which garnered the attention of everyone in the place. I couldn't tell who was enjoying it more, Sophia or Natalia.

Whatever Sophia had done time for, it was a waste having talent like hers off the street. Watching events unfold, I cursed that I didn't know exactly how to use her. I now had access to Natalia and contemplated having drugs planted and staging a fake bust to give Jason his leverage, but feared something going wrong. With others, it didn't matter. They were all expendable. But part of me felt sorry for Natalia, and maybe something else toward Sophia.

In spite of her thinking I was some dude named Chris, Sophia was too close; close enough to see behind the illusions I wielded. Too close to Collette that she could hurt me if she chose. These days, I refused to be hurt.

With the music not to his liking, Penny decided to bounce. He gave his boys a pound then departed the VIP alone. Having learned some of his habits, I found this odd. His girl Natalia didn't seem to notice, feeling nothing but good vibrations from the bubbly, as she continued to dance up on Sophia. The large brother I remembered from Houston, her assistant or whatever, tried talking her down off the tiny table, but she rejected his pleas. Pissy drunk she was, but nothing blackmail worthy. Despite Penny being no more than a distraction from my real mission, I decided to follow him for a second. Besides, Natalia wasn't going anywhere.

Eyes red from herb and whatnot, the rapper took a deep breath as our elevator descended to the casino level. I looked different from our last encounter, but kept my phone to my ear just in case, engaged in an imaginary conversation with a late night booty call.

"C'mon, just let me come by for a sec. I just wanna talk, s'all. Nah, I ain't been drinkin'," I cooed to an audience of none. Overhearing my false and pathetic game, he shook his head once, but never looked back. I trailed behind him, watching him as he signed autographs on the casino floor, including one on the enhanced breast of one of the beautiful neon-angel hostesses. He craved the adulation. Impressive how this fearsome man had risen from the gutters of Miami to the boardrooms of New York and into America's hearts. I'd seen Jason do similar things with his artists at On-Phire Records, but not to this degree. Not on this level. Jason would've given up his testicles to have someone like Penny on his roster.

Just as in the club upstairs, Stratus's casino had areas equally designated for its high rollers. In this VIP section, Penny Antnee only had to flash his exclusive Aire Card, transparent except for its magnetic strip, to gain entry beyond the velvet ropes. When I reached the floor manager, I ended my fake conversation, digging through my pockets for my own Aire Card, as if I'd done it a hundred times before.

"Mister . . . *Spielberg*?" he asked, as the full name on my card made him do a double-take.

"Adopted," I answered as if more than mildly irritated. "Bet you don't give Lenny Kravitz a hard time like this. I get so tired of the anti-Semitic bullshit."

"No, sir . . . I . . ." the floor manager tried to offer as he saw his career flashing before his eyes. "*Ahem*. My apologies. Enjoy, Mister Spielberg."

As Elvis Spielberg of the impressive account balance and over-the-top name, I roamed around the various tables with impunity, putting a few thousand down at roulette, so I could observe Penny at a nearby craps table.

Athletes always want to be rappers and vice versa. Both groups think they're invincible. Both groups like to party like rock stars. Both think they're ballers. Athletes like to drop freestyles when they really shouldn't, and rappers like to own teams. Where one group is likely to be hanging, you'll find the other. A lot of overlap, especially in this town.

I say this because tonight was no exception. At least three NBA ballers, a European footballer, and five NFL players were milling about, trying their luck around us. At Penny's table, he was involved in a friendly competition with a wide receiver I'd caught on *Best Damn Sports Show*

Period before. Besides trying to see who could drink the most complimentary drinks, they were vying for who could lose the most money, too, dice rolling recklessly the more shit they talked and the more they drank. The neon angels, sensing big tips and maybe a rescue from this place if they played their cards right, hovered nearby with less saintly things on their minds.

I'd seen it all before and quickly grew bored, deciding to leave Penny Antnee and get back on mission. Back at the elevator to take me upstairs to Soar, I passed three men as they exited.

"Excuse me," I said as I accidentally bumped into one of them.

I boarded as before, fixing my eyes on the numbers and minding my own business when I felt a presence.

The Haitian brother from Penny's entourage. I would come to learn his name. He's who I'd bumped.

Golden pendant on his chain looked like a hairy wolfman from one of those old Lon Chaney Jr. films, although I just couldn't see him as a fan of old black and whites.

He stood there, staring at me. Confused. Like when you see someone you know, but the setting and context is all wrong. Like that person you went to high school with that graduated a year earlier, and you see them years later, but in a different city.

Except I never went to school with his ass—and I didn't ever want to see him again.

Made the mistake of making eye contact.

Caught slipping.

He was opening his mouth to say something when I pushed the button to close the doors. For a second, nothing happened.

"Hold up," he called out, flashing golden fangs for fronts in his mouth.

I realized the elevator wasn't closing because I'd pushed the wrong button, instead keeping the doors open longer. I quickly corrected that.

"Ay! Hold up, man!" he yelled, not sure what his mind was telling him, yet still getting worked up over it.

I tried remaining calm, but my finger pounded the button like I was trying to break it. I heard his hands slapping against the doors just as they shut. A second faster and he would've been in the elevator with me and I might have had to do something I vowed never to do again.

Rather than continuing up top, I pushed another button to stop on the sixth floor. Before the door opened, I removed my jacket and neck tie in an attempt to change my appearance yet again. When it got to the sixth floor, I pushed a few more random buttons. Bounding into the hallway, I spied the floor was empty. Still, the hotel's security monitors were capturing everything I was doing. I was no fool.

And the adjacent elevator was rising.

I could hear its whirring gears as it approached. It was him. Had to be.

He'd waited to see what floor mine had stopped on first. Should've stayed on.

Nothing like running down the hall to attract unwanted attention; I began walking away as if looking for my room number, with key card in hand. I didn't dare look back.

The elevator doors opened. Someone stepped off.

I kept walking. Maybe a little faster, but still walking. I rounded the corner as heavy feet roamed behind me. Searching.

From my pocket, I fished out my cell. Not a lot in place tonight to deal with this, I called the only person I could.

"Need a favor," I muttered.

"I ain't installing no more cameras," the valet said shrilly, no doubt enjoying a brisk business outside.

"Stop talking and listen," I said, briefly losing the "Harlemisms" I'd used for his benefit. I saw a stairwell up ahead. "You seen the dreaded-up Haitian with Penny Antnee?"

"Loup Garou?" he answered. Wasn't expecting French out of his mouth.

"What?"

"Loup Garou, the Haitian Werewolf, son," he repeated. Now I knew what that pendant and those stupid gold fangs were all about. "That's what he calls himself. Penny got his crazy ass as part of his crew. Nigga think he can rap. I just say he crazy. What about him?"

"Call your girl on staff. Need security to stop him. He might be strapped."

"Word?" he remarked, sounding amused. "You wanna fuck with Penny good, huh? When you need this?"

"Immediately," I answered as I reached the stairwell and quietly opened the door. I think I'd put some distance between us.

"Man, I'm in the middle of a shift. How about later tonight?"

"Do that shit now," I urged as I bounded up the stairs two at a time. "He's running around on the sixth floor. If they hurry, they might catch him. Somebody could get hurt." Wasn't quite sure if it would be him or me if it came to it, but I didn't dare show up on anyone's arrest records.

"Another bonus?"

"Duh," I replied, hanging up as I walked out onto the eighth floor, merging with a crowd of folk on my way back to the elevators.

One less tense ride up this time, I exited with everyone else at Soar. The place was at capacity now, so I stood in the winding line to patiently wait my turn, in spite of my wristband. As I rested against the wall, I overheard someone commenting on "some rapper dude" being thrown to the floor by security and escorted from the building. It was already showing up on Twitter.

Little solace, as I still didn't have anything on Natalia to use. Strange that while despising Jason, some part of me still hated disappointing him.

A group of partygoers drew attention as they escaped the excitement inside, either done for the night or simply taking the party elsewhere. When I heard Natalia's name being screamed out further up the line, I perked up.

She was leaving—arm in arm with Sophia.

Legs striding as if on someone's runway, the bow on her dress was still there, waiting to be unwrapped.

I made sure Sophia saw me. Holding her new-found friend up as they staggered by, she winked at me. No words; just a look saying, *I got this*.

Extraordinary.

I nodded, letting them pass with nary a word on my part.

As the elevator closed with them in it, I knew where they were headed.

And I knew where I needed to be.

Chapter 15

Chapter 15

Back at my hotel room, with my laptop powered up, everything was a go. My jacket lay
tossed on the back of my chair. Shoes kicked off,
I rolled up my sleeves. The hairs on the back of
my neck stood on end as the electronic world
before me sprang to life once more. In another
life, I probably would've been serving abroad in
military intelligence or the CIA. But I wasn't that
guy. I came up on a path less traveled. A dark,
winding road with hairpin turns and sudden pit-
falls rarely seen until it was too late.

The camera installed in the bedroom smoke
detector of Natalia's suite still worked. Someone
was in the living room, but I couldn't make out
the figures.

Nothing was happening in Penny Antnee's
suite. Downstairs blowing his wad . . . of another
sort, no doubt.

During this lull, I took my phone and down-
loaded the photo I'd taken of Katelyn McMahon

back at Soar. Knowing I wasn't the only one with a camera phone, time was of the essence for such a shot. Once I sent the jpeg on its way, I waited for a response. The recipient replied almost immediately.

That looks like Vegas. I knew you'd be out there!

You said you needed something.

Yeah. But this ain't my normal demographic. And no-singing, no-actin' white girls getting drunk in clubs ain't new. You couldn't get Natalia, or Halle Berry at least?

I'm throwing you a bone. If you don't like, I'm sure TMZ will. Check out what Katelyn's best friend is busy doing with her boyfriend in the background.

Oh! Snap! I missed that.

That's what I'm here for. To illuminate things.

I owe you.

I know. Out.

I went back to monitoring the pair of suites over at Stratus, drinking from my bottle of Voss while I rested my feet atop the desk. Sophia and Natalia finally entered the bedroom, where I could see them better. Knowing for certain where they were, I closed the window to the feed in Penny Antnee's suite and enlarged the screen to Natalia's instead.

Through my cyber looking glass, I peered into a world of silent seduction. Having no audio really sucked. Natalia and Sophia danced around the room, spinning in circles. Natalia was out of her sandals, making her noticeably shorter as she reached up to drape her arms around Sophia's neck. She reminded me of one of those drunken sorority girls, probably slurring her words while professing her undying love for her best friend.

One final spin and Sophia was done. She pried Natalia's hands away as she gently lowered her onto the bed. I remembered viewing a similar scene, but with Natalia dancing before Penny Antnee in nothing but a towel. Now Natalia was the spectator.

And Sophia, the performer.

She said something to Natalia. Made her laugh and gush all bubbly-like. Then she bent over, pressing her lips on Natalia's.

Like she'd done to me.

Was that it? Her way inside both of us, spreading her will like an infection from a simple kiss?

Natalia didn't jerk away or fight the kiss either. She embraced it. Like she'd been waiting . . . and wanting. I rocked back in my seat, smiling at the breakthrough.

When Sophia stood back up, Natalia's face hovered there as if begging for another kiss. Sophia told her something as she began a sensual dance for her entertainment. Slowly and methodically, Sophia wound her body like a corkscrew. Just out of reach of Natalia, Sophia's ass swooped and swayed like something out of a dancehall in Kingston. Natalia was unable to stand, so she sat and tolerated the tease.

When Sophia got too close, Natalia lunged forward. She grasped the back of Sophia's thighs, holding on firmly so as to not fall over. Natalia's hands then snaked their way under the bow at the back of Sophia's dress. Steadying herself, Natalia nuzzled her head under the front. Sophia made a face equal parts joy and surprise as Natalia fished for her sweet spot. I watched Sophia's hands rest atop the mound that was Natalia's head as it bobbed and probed beneath the silk dress I'd bought. As Natalia ate her out, Sophia pulled the working head deeper between her legs. Still in her heels, Sophia's toned legs showed no signs of fatigue as she began winding and grinding again, against Natalia's hunting mouth and tongue, no doubt.

As sweet little Natalia asserted herself, the back of Sophia's dress popped up in view of my camera. Nails dug into Sophia's bare ass cheeks, clawing then releasing them in a sensual massage. No panties on that pretty brown ass. Knew it.

Sophia hiked her dress up completely, providing me an unmistakable view of Natalia's face. I watched her tongue as it disappeared from view within the folds Sophia's hot flesh between gasps for air. Sophia performed as if she knew she was being videoed, gyrating seductively as Natalia continued to lick, probe, and taste her. My dick rose from the spectacle as I imagined Sophia knowing my eyes were focused on her.

And that she wanted to please me even more than Natalia.

She shed her dress, pulling it over her head before throwing it on the floor. As she removed her bra, Natalia paused to marvel at her body. Natalia said something, but I was unable to read her lips. With my swollen dick throbbing even more, I imagined it was something beautiful and poetic. She was a lyricist, after all.

Sophia joined Natalia on the bed, allowing Natalia to slide next to her. Natalia kissed softly over the curve of Sophia's ass then across her thighs and up her stomach as Sophia turned over. Sophia touched herself, stimulating her clit and caressing her breasts as the moment overcame her too. As they rolled across the enlarged bed, Sophia wound up atop Natalia, where she reversed and straddled Natalia's face. Natalia's arms reached around Sophia's thighs, securing her in place, as if on an amusement park ride. Sophia bit her lip as she came. With her face obscured by Sophia's orgasmic sweetness, I watched the singer's legs writhe atop the sheets, as if she were falling, with no end in sight.

Sophia bent over atop Natalia and ripped her dress open, leaving her exposed on a layer of black fabric. Unlike Sophia, Natalia wore a thong. With Natalia still gorging on her, Sophia returned the favor, pulling the black fabric aside and dipping her tongue into Natalia's exposed, smooth pussy. Natalia rocked uncontrollably at Sophia's oral mastery, legs still writhing in that never-ending tumble and cascade of emotions, completing the numeral of the sacred sixty-nine, two folded into one.

As the video feed continued, I sat riveted in my chair, both envious and desperate to imagine the sensations denied me by both distance and digital.

The *U.S. Icon* winner had more to her than the show's producers could've imagined.

Much more.

She was a star.

And Jason had what he wanted.

Chapter 16

For hours they went on, pleasures heaped upon one another by virtue of the intimate knowledge that only another woman could possess.

And I continued to watch.

In the end, Sophia was reduced to tending to a weary and spent Natalia, going as far as wiping her down with a warm towel before departing at daybreak.

Ragged and sore from sitting too long, I stretched before pushing the button for the recording to end. I walked over to the fridge, fighting back a yawn, and grabbed another bottled water before I began edits of my presentation to Jason.

I placed a call to Sophia, anxious to see how she was doing.

"Where are you?"

"Caught a cab," she muttered. She had to be exhausted.

"Are you okay?"

"I'll live. Wasn't half bad," she chuckled. "Told you I was willing to do anything."

"That you did."

"You saw?"

"Yes," I admitted.

"Chris?"

"Yeah?"

"Can I come by your room? I . . . I just don't feel like being alone. Thought maybe we could cuddle."

Damn her. Images of her and Natalia were too recent. Too raw on my mind. I wanted her right now in the worst of ways.

"I'm working right now," I said as I rewound to a still shot of Sophia. Zoomed in on her face when Natalia's mouth first touched her down there. Saw the ecstasy. "Go to your room. Get some sleep. I'll check on you a little later."

"Are you sure?"

"Yeah. I got too much work to do."

"Y'know . . . I could just lay there and watch you. Promise I won't make a sound."

"No. You would be a distraction. Get some sleep. I'll check up on you."

I hung up after that. Doing my best to handle her like any other pawn. Girl was too close. The sooner she and Vegas were behind me, the better. For now I had to focus on the client. A client that expected results.

I called Jason, half expecting his voice mail at this time of morning.

"It's me," I said upon his answering.

"Nice of you to call me, Truth," Jason North answered, not seeming the least bit disturbed.

"You made it?"

"Yes, we're here. Major press coverage, so On-Phire Records will be representing. Did you pick up that suit for me yet?" he asked, fearing a possible wiretap, I suppose.

"I got it."

"Incredible. Absolutely incredible," he crowed. "You never cease to amaze me, son. Where did you buy it? Men's Wearhouse?"

"No, it's Italian. Tailor-made," I said as I began obscuring Sophia's face throughout the video. I rationalized that it was to protect me, in the event someone recognized her and made her talk. Yeah. That's my story.

"The quality's that good?"

"Impeccable. It should fit your needs rather nicely," I answered as I manipulated the software to zoom in on Natalia's face during a choice moment to help with authenticity.

"Good. When can I see it?"

"Tonight. I won't be in town much longer. Got places to be."

"You're not staying for the awards?"

"You know me. I'm not one for that kind of attention. Name the place and I'll be there."

"Splendid. Why don't you come by the mixer we're holding tonight at Caesars Palace."

"Okay."

"Oh, and no need for theatrics or sneaking up on me. Security will be on alert. My heart can't take all that. Besides, we have nothing but love for you within our family, son."

"Keep the love. I've seen the results of your *love*."

"One day you'll see the light."

"That day arrived long ago. Or don't you remember?" I asked, hinting at things Jason would rather forget.

"Just bring the suit, Truth."

"I will."

Hating loose ends, I got back to work on the video for Jason. When the edits were complete hours later, I burned a DVD then took a look through the camera I had hidden in Sophia's room. With the lamp beside her bed still on, she slept soundly. Passed out atop the covers, still clothed in her dress. I contemplated her earlier request for comfort and companionship, but quickly flicked off the video feed instead. I was in dire need of some sleep, which I would get right after my shower.

***

It took the faint buzz of a missed call on my cell to wake me from my slumber. I fumbled in the darkened room to find it, seeing that it was a call from Jason. He could wait.

But Sophia couldn't.

Even up to this moment, she'd consumed my dreams, far more appealing than the usual monsters that dwelled in the dark recesses of my mind, waiting for me to fall victim to their torment. I pulled myself from the plush confines of the exclusive Westin Heavenly Bed, the light escaping through the tiny gap between the curtains telling me it was close to midday.

Dragging myself to the desk, I turned on my laptop once again. Bypassing messages in my inbox, I activated my link to Sophia's video feed.

Nothing.

I tried the link one more time, thinking I had a bad connection.

Still nothing.

My phone rang again, forcing me to check it. It was another call from Jason. Ignoring him, I quickly threw on some clothes to check on Sophia.

When I reached her hotel room, I knocked, but nobody answered. I began to suspect something was wrong. I knocked again, contemplating using the spare room key. Just as I reached in my pocket, she showed, lazily bopping down the hallway, wearing warm-ups that showed off her abs again.

"Where've you been?" I asked, removing my hand from the extra key to her room. I tried hiding my concern about her camera not transmitting, as well as my concern for her well-being.

"Took you up on the spa treatment. Needed some stress relief after last night," she answered with the insinuation of my reluctance to help a sister out. If only she knew how close I had come to giving in. "Was going to call you to see if you wanted to join me for breakfast, but I figured you had better things to do."

"I apologize if I came across as rude, Sophia. Just trying to keep things professional."

"Uh-huh. Want to come in? I mean, since you're paying for the room."

In spite of my concerns, no dangers awaited us upon entering. Her dress sat on the chair where she'd taken it off, probably still enhanced with Natalia's scent on it. The tiny camera I'd hidden to observe her sat dismantled atop the TV. She said nothing of it, preferring to leave it out there for me to see.

I sat in the chair near the window, watching her step out of her Nikes first. She was about to shower, and I simply smiled, figuring to go through her stuff while she did so.

Habit.

"Did you get what you wanted?" she asked as she removed her warm-up bottoms and panties in unison. Oblivious to the view she was giving anyone who could see in her room from the window behind me, she glistened, courtesy of the fresh oil from her spa session.

"Yes. Thank you."

"How about on me?"

"What?"

Still half-clothed, she walked over to her purse, that model walk of hers returning in spite of nothing covering her bottom half. She reached in the purse and hurled the wallet containing her driver's license at me. I snatched it from the air before it caught me in the eye.

"Since you want to know about me too," she said, finally acknowledging the camera she'd found.

As I looked at the driver's license, she continued undressing, disrupting my focus. Sophia Williams of Santa Monica, CA, it read. When I looked up, she was totally nude.

Exposed.

"I'm no amateur," she offered as my eyes went from hers down to the tiny heart tattoo visible just below her bikini line. "Done some things in the past for a guy I thought I was in love with. I was willing to do anything for him. Kind of like you."

"Oh?"

"Yeah," she breathed, letting the single syllable linger ominously in the air. "Except he was a crackhead. He's responsible for my legal troubles back in Cali. Beautiful man, he was. Cunning as fuck. Turned me on so much. It was a thrill just being around him, sharing the moments. Made me wet like you wouldn't believe."

"All that reminiscing making you wet now?"

"Want to find out?" she uttered, stopping at the bathroom's edge, her action on pause, daring me to push play.

"Were you telling the truth when you said you'd do anything for me?"

"Yes."

From my back pocket, I retrieved an envelope. I walked over to her and put it in her hand. "Time to go back to Dallas," I said calmly.

"Is that all you want from me, Chris? Really?" She was close enough for me to smell the menthol and lavender oils on her body. Their mix with her natural pheromones set my pulse racing.

"Yes," I replied, a supreme act on my part. "Thank you . . . for everything."

"Suit yourself," she snapped. "I'm going take a shower then I'll be out of your hair. Close the door on your way out. And take your camera with you."

Clutching Sophia's camera in my hand, I obeyed and left for my room. While I had it on my mind, I called Francis the valet, figuring he'd be back at work after last night's shift.

"I need you to pull the cameras 'n stuff. Put them in a garbage bag and dump them out back where we discussed," I instructed as I moved down the hall on my floor.

"Got what you needed, kid?" he asked.

"No," I replied with the simplest of lies. Didn't need him blabbing or bragging around the casino. "You still get your bonus though," I offered.

"Bonuses," he corrected. "Both of them. Remember? That Loup Garou shit."

"I remember." I sighed.

"Yeah, that's what's up." He chuckled. "Keep at Penny. Rep for the NYC, son. You'll catch him slippin'."

"No doubt."

"Hey, I gotta run. Diddy just pulled up in his Bentley. Nigga a good tipper. *Is he who you working for?*" Francis guessed in a hushed whisper.

"Can't talk about that. Handle your business, kid," I extolled. "Just don't forget to get rid of those cameras."

"I won't."

"Thanks."

"No prob. Peace."

Upon entering, I decided to see what was videoed from Penny Antnee's room. Just in case there
was something useful.

It was black at first, making me think it had
been found like Sophia's. But as I rewound it,
images began to form.

"What the fuck," I said aloud as I suddenly
stopped the recording from last night. I backed
up by a few minutes then pushed play.

Penny Antnee was displayed in all his glory,
pounding away on his sexual conquest, who lay
sprawled face down beneath him on the bed. Unlike Natalia's room, this one had audio.

"You like that shit, don'tcha?" Penny yelled,
sweat evident on his tatted-up body. I could've
rewound further, as they'd been going at it a
while.

Definitely bonus material for me to work with.

Rather than continuing, I stopped. I looked
around my room, feeling something was off, even
though I had been gone a short time. I thought
again about Sophia discovering her camera as
hairs rose on the back of my neck again.

Paranoia was sometimes an ally.

I quickly gathered my things and packed up, wondering if someone was watching me, just as I was apt to do.

I decided to return to Sophia's room below to better keep an eye on her while I remained in Vegas.

"Change of plans," I said when Sophia opened her door. She wore a bath towel now, her wet hair slicked back and still dripping. I quickly forced my way past her, bags and all. "Feel like attending a party tonight?" I asked.

"Not if I have to sleep with somebody again," she answered smartly.

"Only me," I stated, my mask dissolving. "Only me."

"I could do that," she said with a devilish smirk. She slammed the door shut behind her and undid her robe.

Chapter 17

"Are you sure you're not pawning me off on somebody this time?" she asked, her hand playing inside mine. It cost me another dress, but Sophia accompanied me to PURE nightclub inside Caesars Palace.

"I promise," I replied, squeezing her soft hand for emphasis before bringing it up to my lips, where I kissed the back of her knuckles. We had the look of lovers—or a pair that had hooked up. This was Vegas, after all. It was a ruse based deep in truth, with roots of lust and passion fed by our short time together.

And lust and passion have been the downfall of many a person.

As we moved closer to club security, screening for tonight's special event, I tried ignoring the memories and feelings her touch evoked.

I slipped my hand inside her robe, pressing into the small of her back. I played on, her body trembling, as though pressure points on her back were keys on a piano, her sultry voice the melody in perfect tune.

"Chris, I've wanted to feel you inside me since we first met," she confessed under interrogation by my tongue in her ear. "Don't make me wait any longer," she whispered as I backed her against the door she'd just closed.

I kissed her neck, tasting the fresh, soapy dew from her shower. Dug my hands into her damp hair as I pulled her face to mine, kissing deeply, tasting and sucking her wanton tongue as she dropped her robe.

Sophia undid my pants and yanked them down along with my boxers. Turnabout. Left me naked from the waist down, as she'd been when I was here earlier. Back when I was still thinking and calculating rather than feeling.

Thought takes up too much of my life.

Sex is the only time thoughts aren't necessary.

Our bodies converged, all that chaotic, volatile energy combusting as we tussled. My shirt, pulled over my head then thrown aside. Sophia biting deeply into my neck. My hands palming her ass as I lifted her effortlessly. Her feeding me her breast and my nibbling as if it were a delicacy.

"Mmm, harder, Chris. Bite it," she pled as if Chris were the reality. The figment obliged, sucking on it until arriving at her plump nipple, where I playfully took it in my teeth. She slapped up against me harder, shuddering as she came.

She led me to the chair I'd been in before and sat me down. My dick hungered, and there would be no turning back. She went over to her purse to retrieve a condom. I stroked myself, watching her and wondering just how potent that pussy was.

Placing the ringed condom in her mouth, she returned, dropping to her knees as she slid it down my dick with no hands. The warm sensation of her breath through the latex made me flinch.

"Mmmm," I groaned.

"Do I make you hot? Do I turn you on?" she coaxed, rising to her feet as she straddled me.

"Yes," I answered, smiling as she slid onto me.

"Do you want it, baby?" she inquired as she began riding.

"Absolutely."

Sophia grasped the back of the chair behind me, working her hips with each bounce. She whipped her head around feverishly, causing her wet strands to land across her face.

I grabbed her waist, slamming her harder and harder onto me with each bounce. As I impaled her, she screamed in ecstasy, tremors delivering another gush onto my lap.

"Damn, you are so good. Don't stop," I begged.

"I won't," she said, breathing heavily.

We rushed toward that point, the place where time stands still, gravity ceases, toes curl, eyes roll, and nothing makes sense other than that singular, unique moment.

"I . . . I'm . . ." I stuttered, sweat covering my brow. I was fighting it, but going down in flames, rushing to my eventual end.

"Mmmm. Let it go. Let it all go. Yesss."

And I did.

I heaved upward, slamming inside her a final time as my legs went stiff, blowing a mighty load that jolted her from the high ground she'd held in our intimate encounter. Having delivered me to this point, Sophia held me close as she tried to steady her breathing. Her sweaty breasts rose and fell, gradually decreasing in their intensity each time.

"Mmm. You make me cum harder than him, baby," she panted, referring to her ex. The one with the addictive personality. The one who'd commanded her in all sorts of unseemly things.

I was no better.

As she collapsed in my arms, I wondered if she had traded one addiction for one perhaps far worse.

"Chris?" Sophia called out, releasing my hand and severing my connection to past events shared by us. I was back in the now, and facing the club's security.

"Sir, it's a special function tonight. Sorry," he said, obviously repeating it due to my daydreaming. My posture tonight projected someone not used to being denied.

"I'm on the list," I calmly announced.

"Your name?"

"Truth North," I mumbled, hating to reveal my true name in public. They say to bind a demon, you only have to know its name then speak it. If Sophia meant me any harm, then . . .

"Thank you, sir," he said, moving aside, as he understood my last name and what it entailed. "Enjoy your evening."

I led Sophia through the main room, where Mark Ronson deejayed. On one of the oversized beds that surrounded the dance floor, Nicole Scherzinger of the Pussycat Dolls engaged in an intense conversation with the producer Smith-Sonian. Probably trying to pry from him one of those exotic, fly tracks he was known to spit out when the mood struck. Even from my early days with On-Phire, he was known as a talented space case. His real name was Jules, a runaway from an upper crust Connecticut family with a musical gift and way too many therapy sessions as a kid.

"Super producer SmithSonian in da house!" Mark Ronson called out on a break beat, upon which SmithSonian paused his conversation with the sultry lead singer long enough to wave at the few intoxicated folks popping bottles of bubbly in his direction.

As I led Sophia by him, he nodded, recognizing me from the old days, only because I allowed it this time. He was completely clueless that I had been standing next to him last night in the lobby of Stratus.

"Ain't seen you in a while, boy. The pyramids are definitely in alignment with the stars tonight," SmithSonian yelled. Ms. Pussycat Doll put a finger in her ear to shield it from his volume.

"Good to see you too, Jules," I responded, bringing a frown to his face. Not in front of his potential clients. "This is my girlfriend, Tiffany."

Sophia waved. He waved back.

"Never saw you as the type to settle down, boy," he said, leaning in so I could hear. "Or have anyone in your life, for that matter."

"Times change, man. Even for me," I answered. "I'll let you handle your business. It was good seeing you again."

I patted him on the shoulder, allowing him to continue his negotiations as we moved on.

"Tiffany? You could've picked a better name."

"Get over it. I just felt like messing with Jules."

"If you have this much weight in these circles, then why all the top secret stuff at Soar?" Sophia quizzed.

"Because I'm not a high-profile person. That's not how I operate," I said over the loud music. She raised an eyebrow, amused.

I received a text on my phone and read it. "Why don't you mingle for a second? I'll be back."

"Only if you dance with me before we leave."

I opened my mouth to protest.

"Just once," she quickly declared. "Want to see if you're as good out there on the floor as you are in bed."

"Okay," I relented. "But we never quite made it to the bed. Remember?"

"I'm clairvoyant. I see into the future," she said smartly, as I told myself I was never again doing anything except dance with her.

Leaving Sophia to whatever trouble she could get into, I took the twisting staircase to the terrace, per Jason's text message. I tapped my suit jacket once to ensure the disc was still there. Emerging upstairs, I admired the rooftop view of The Strip as the nearby heating lamp provided comfort from the cool desert air. Stunning to just take it in, even if for a second.

"Tell Jason I'm here," I said to the security camped outside his private bungalow. Laughter came from it, along with cigar smoke. Fine rolled Havanas, by the smell.

When the burly bodyguard entered, he mumbled something. All the energy suddenly left, except for Jason's voice.

Just like old times. If they weren't afraid of me, they simply hated me. Things like that, I missed.

Through the dissipating haze, I saw my dear uncle seated in the center. Instead of his usual assortment of flunkies, he held court with record label execs. No wonder they were isolated on high from the usual assortment below. Like shit, money flowed downhill, and they were certainly the ones raking it in atop the artists' heads.

He kept me waiting a moment longer, giving him time to excuse himself.

"You look well," Jason uttered, looking every bit the executive. E! Entertainment Television was on hand, so he was probably aiming for camera time.

"Thank you. What now?"

"Would you like some champagne, or your usual whiskey sour?" he said as he began to motion for one of the waiters.

"Nope. Just want to do this and jet."

"Very well then. Come on. Let's go to the Red Room downstairs. I'm not too thrilled about those open spaces when conducting business. You might have someone in one of those buildings filming us."

I smirked. "Why would I do that?" I asked. "We're family. Remember?"

"Whatever," he replied, borrowing my usual retort.

We took the glass elevator to the Red Room, the true VIP section in this most special of nightclubs. As soon as we exited, I noticed Mariah Carey and Diddy chilling along with a few comedians. In this area, it was about not being star-struck or caught up in the hype. You had a chance to just unwind and exhale, without cameras or partygoers searching for something. The stuff overheard in this area alone could net me a month's material for my Internet client, but I would be violating a sacred trust.

Diddy removed his toothpick long enough to give Jason dap as we strolled by. Jason leaned over, giving Mariah a kiss on the cheek, along with a few fond words. The comedians cracked jokes about the lifespan of the average On-Phire artist, to which Jason chuckled and blew it off. Unknown to them and off their radar, I was ignored.

In one of the small reserved alcoves, a portable DVD player rested on the tiny mahogany table. I followed Jason to it, retrieving the disc from my jacket.

"I hope your plans for it are worth it," I muttered, suddenly wondering if Natalia was in attendance tonight.

Stroking his goatee, Jason chimed, "I give a damn about Natalia. This is for the future, dear boy. Leverage." He inserted the disc I'd edited and stared at the images. "Damn. She's cutting loose, isn't she?"

"Sorry there's no audio, but you had me on a short timetable," I offered, imagining again what sensual sounds were present that night.

Ignoring me, he inquired, "Who's the woman with her?"

"Someone random."

"Uh-huh," he scoffed. "Then why is her face blurred?"

"Because you didn't pay for her. You wanted something on Natalia, and that's what I delivered."

"Shit. She's someone famous?" he asked about the obscured Sophia anyway, evidently aroused and not expecting an answer. "With a body like that, I'll bet she is. Damn."

"I've done what I'm supposed to, so I'd appreciate your doing the same."

"Fair enough, Truth," he responded, extending his hand for me to shake it. I declined. "I'm looking forward to more good stuff from you."

"Not if I can help it."

Knowing the worm was at least good for his money, I left him with the product and returned to the main room. It took a while to find Sophia, but when I did, she was just about to take to the dance floor with some Italian guy. I ignored him and pressed on.

"C'mon, let's go," I said, grabbing her by the arm. She wriggled free, adjusting the top of her strapless orange dress. I gave a stern glance to Fabio, or whatever his name was, telling him to move on.

"You forgot your promise already," Sophia barked.

"We have a plane to catch. Stop playing."

"I'm not playing. One dance, then we can go."

It was too long in one place. Too many people knew I was here. But against my better judgment, I obliged.

We danced to a roaring master-mix by Mark
Ronson, close to one another, as Sophia showed
me what she was working with. Time slipped by
as I gave in to the rush of the moment. Driving
bass and Sophia's moving hips could be most
persuasive. Besides, the flight back to Dallas
didn't leave for several hours. In the middle of
business, I found myself having fun.

Sophia wrapped her arms around my neck,
slowing her movement during the break in the
music. She wanted to kiss me again. As her lips
came closer, she abruptly stopped their progress.

"Company. Six o'clock," she said, gazing over
my shoulder. I whipped her around in a turn so I
could have a better look.

Jason.

He glad-handed everyone as he approached
us, the faux smile never leaving his face.

"I thought you were leaving, Truth."

"It's a free country. Felt like a dance."

"True that, nephew," he teased. Slang always
sounded so hollow, so false whenever he attempted it. "You didn't tell me you had a date
though. Jules—er, SmithSonian said he'd run
into you earlier, so I came down to see if you
were still here. Forgive me for being a doting
uncle rather than a music mogul just this once."

Crushed Ice 131

"He's your uncle?" Sophia asked. I could tell from her expression that she recognized who Jason North was.

"That I am, my dear," Jason replied for me. He took her hand in his and kissed it. "Jason North at your service."

"Tiffany," she stated in kind, remembering the name I'd used with SmithSonian. Good girl.

"Have we met before?" he asked, as if the memory was on the tip of his tongue. In actuality, the memory was on the tip of his finger when he'd pressed "play" on the DVD player.

"I don't think so," Sophia replied. Again, something triggered the hairs on the back of my neck. Time to go.

"Truth has impeccable taste whenever he lets others see it," Jason stated.

Sophia blushed, although I wasn't sure if she was faking it for effect.

"Is there something you wanted? Or do you just feel like fu—"

I froze. Over the throng of people in the main room, a face stood out. I'd only spent all night looking at it when it wasn't buried between Sophia's legs. As she planted false Hollywood kisses on the cheeks of partygoers, she was working her way in our direction.

"Natalia's here. We have to go. Now," I whispered, grasping Sophia by the arm.

"Why the rush? I can have a couple of bottles of Veuve Clicquot sent over."

"Maybe another time," I offered dismissively as I spirited Sophia away before Jason could sink his fangs in her, or Natalia could see us.

We wormed our way through the crowd, intent on getting out as soon as possible. Fate was on our side, for we'd just exited PURE through one door when Penny Antnee and his boys rolled up to enter the club. That included Loup Garou, who only saw the back of my head as Sophia and I headed in the opposite direction.

Instead of sharing my relief, Sophia chose to pepper me with question after question during the cab ride to the airport. I had no respite.

"Truth," she called out. "That's really your name?"

"Yeah."

"Wow. Like, 'the truth will set you free,' or truth or dare?"

"Something like that."

"And Jason North from On-Phire Records is your . . . uncle?"

"Yeah," I answered wearily as I stared at my reflection in the cab window, a reflection that shared more than a passing resemblance to Jason. I was thinking about the final contemptuous gaze I'd shared with him in PURE. The one Sophia didn't see. "We're family."

Chapter 18

Way Back . . .

"Who is the boy's father?" he asked. "Or do you even know?"

She slapped him. Straight up pasted her hand to his face. "How dare you," my mother spat. I was astounded by her rage, but kept my head down. Grown folks' business. I remember staring at the hardwood floor to his office and thinking how pristine it was.

The place looked more like a house, with its inviting porch and black wrought iron fence outside, than a law office. Although my mother had told me of the city often enough, that didn't prepare me. New Orleans was different—equal parts magic and madness, triumph and tragedy. More fairy tale than Hollywood even.

What lessons had driven my mother from here?

"A man can't ask a simple question?" my mother's brother asked as he rubbed his reddened cheek. "I haven't seen you since you ran off. Now you show up with this boy. I only discovered you were on the soaps because somebody out here recognized you. Can't say what you were doing before that when you were in New Mexico. Wait. I take that back. I know some of what you were doing in New Mexico . . . which brings me back to my original question."

"He's my son. I was pregnant with him before I got to New Mexico. And that's all that should matter," she said steadfastly, her hand on my shoulder as she resisted slapping him again. He looked at me curiously, then back at my mother.

"How old are you, son?" he asked me as he came closer. He made me nervous. When I answered, he stared at me longer. Made me wish we'd stayed in California and never took the Greyhound here, despite how bad things had become.

"We were living out of the car. Then it got impounded. I couldn't think of anyone else. We . . . I need help," she said, her voice trailing off. I listened to how she skipped over some of the darker aspects of our ordeal. They'd begun to take a toll on her mind. She saw things that weren't there, and rarely slept. Over the years, I would come to comprehend them more thoroughly.

"You should have been called me, Leila. I'm doing things now."

"The legal business suits you, huh?"

"Not this. It keeps the bills paid, but if you're not knee deep in the politics or ambulance chasing of this place, you can only progress so far. They can keep their old machinery. I'm talking about a new way, using the rich musical history of this city as my tool instead. All these local rappers are on to something, my dear. I have a silent investor with contacts in places I'm unfamiliar with. I'm heading a record label," he said, beaming with pride.

"Want a job, son?"

"Sir?" I stated, remembering my manners.

"Jason, we just need a place to stay for a few weeks. Just so I can get on my feet. Leave him out of this."

"Look at you," he jeered. "You look like shit, Leila. Y'all need far more than a few weeks."

He looked at me again. "Son, are you in school?"

"Yes," I said, lying.

"You're lying," he said as he glanced at my mother again. "You know how I know?"

"No, sir."

"Because I'm a liar," he answered. "And a better one than you. Don't ever forget that. Now, let me ask you again, do you want a job?"

"Yes, sir."

"Good," he said, placing his hand on the shoulder opposite the one my mother was touching. An angel on one and a devil on the other. At this moment, I didn't know which was which. "What's your name anyway?"

"Truth."

He rolled his eyes at my mother. "As in, 'the truth will set you free'?"

"Yes, sir. That's what she named me after," I answered, lying again.

"Interesting," he said. He bought it. My mother smiled through her haze, proud. I was learning. "And please stop calling me sir. You can call me Uncle Jason. We're family, after all."

Chapter 19

I dreamed of an old Nissan Altima from pre-Katrina days. The one I drove down Old Gentilly Road in the rain, dodging potholes, with my precious cargo stowed in the trunk. In my rearview mirror, I saw the headlights of the other car that followed me. I jumped around in my dream, going back hours before.

"This yo' fault, North," Melvin, the real money and power behind On-Phire, barked. A dangerous man with a dark soul, his deep, raspy tone scared both of us. Jason was the front for the cameras, but the final decisions came from Melvin, a ruthless killer and not-so-former drug dealer. Jason's law degree gave an air of legitimacy and class to a company that still had its hands dirty when dealing with its artists. Shitty contracts and outright theft were the normal course of business.

"I had nothing to do with this, Melvin!" Jason yelled as he sidestepped around his massive desk to get some distance from his boss. "That cop was wilding out on his own. You know that."

On-Phire's rising star, AK, had been feuding with us, and now he'd wound up shot and killed by an NOPD cop who lost his fucking mind. Real talk, AK had publicly thumbed his nose at the label and made some threats to tell all he knew, but Jason hadn't ordered him taken out—yet. He knew better than to do something like that without Melvin's blessing. Besides, Melvin would've been more discreet and personal if he chose to snuff AK. On top of that, there were rumblings of the feds, or at least the IRS, wanting to take a closer look at the label. Between the public AK/On-Phire feud and the shady business dealings, this was the worst of times.

"Too much attention being brought on us. I don't like that. You trying to put the company in the spotlight. I done told ya about that shit. Nigga need to slow his roll before I slow it for him."

"There's no need for threats," Jason muttered. "Lord knows how successful we've been with your approach. If you had listened to me in the beginning—"

"What the fuck did you say?" Melvin asked, his ebony features contorting into a grimace, like he'd just ingested prune juice. I tensed for my uncle.

"I was just—"

Melvin reached across the desk, backhanding Jason before he could complete his sentence. The reading glasses Jason liked to wear when lecturing someone broke in half from the impact, which left him holding the side of his face in stunned amazement. I think he wanted to cry.

"Thought I wouldn't do that because your nephew here, huh?" Melvin taunted.

The man had only done what I'd felt like doing several times before, but I still felt sorry for Jason. That faint family bond, I guess.

"Next time you want to strut around like a peacock, remember . . . bitches get fucked."

"You . . . you didn't have to do that," Jason spoke brokenly as he looked at me to gauge my reaction. I showed nothing other than a raised eyebrow. It was just the three of us, after hours in Jason's new office on Elysian Fields Boulevard, sparing him some embarrassment.

"I say what I want and I do what I want. You might as well stop your crying." Melvin had moved over to the window, eyeing the storm blowing outside. "Some days I don't know why I keep your ass around."

"Funny, I feel the same way about you," Jason suddenly snarled.

Melvin and I reacted to Jason's change in tone simultaneously.

One of us was too slow.

I don't think Melvin felt the bullet as it split his skull, sending a squirt of blood onto the wall.

"Sir, would you like something to drink?" the flight attendant asked, sparing me from the memory of the remainder of that incident. I stared at her momentarily as I realized where I was.

"Whiskey sour," I replied.

"That will be five dollars."

"Huh?" Oh, yeah. I was in coach. Had forgotten I'd given up my first class seat to Sophia. Hot towel for her, crying babies and crowded overhead bins for me.

"Five dollars. That's the cost of alcoholic beverages."

The student in the middle seat mumbled something about airline rip-offs, although he wasn't of drinking age yet. I hoped I hadn't said anything while I slept.

"Sorry," I offered as I reached in my wallet.

Sophia emerged through the curtain that separated us. Although I had changed into something more casual, she still wore her strapless orange dress. Her lithe form moved as if suspended on air, while her eyes were that of a predator.

"Wish I had a seat next to her," the student whispered. If I were less of a gentleman tonight, he would've had his wish. I smiled with amusement.

I acted nonchalant, preferring that we not communicate during the flight, but she had a hard head. When she came to my row, she stopped, placing her hand on my shoulder as she leaned over.

"Just came to see how you were doing," she said.

"Fine," I replied, not bothering to chastise her. "Just waiting on my drink."

"Missed you."

The plane dropped suddenly then leveled off. Turbulence. The seatbelt sign came on again.

"We'll talk when we land," I said, grateful for the reprieve. After I'd had my drink, I'd be more amenable to what was to come.

"This is it." I sighed as the cab pulled to a stop in front of La Trattoria Lombardi. We were on North Hall, blocks from my place. Although it was midnight, people still ambled about on a night of clubbing. We'd shared the ride from DFW without saying a word to one another. Sophia was making the end of this task rather tortured. I instructed the cabbie to take her on to Collette's.

Once he retrieved my bag from the trunk, I paid him then watched the cab pull away. It only traveled a few feet before screeching to a halt.

Sophia exited, the cabbie quickly popping his trunk again and scurrying over to help her.

"I said I wanted to talk," she called out as the cabbie grabbed her bag for her. "You're acting like this was nothing."

"It's late and I'm tired, Sophia. You should be too."

"What about my money?" she countered, needing an excuse.

"You'll get it tomorrow."

"What do I call you from now on?"

"Chris."

"Even though it's not your name?"

"It is to you."

"But what if I want to call you Truth?"

"Easy," I replied. "Don't. Ever. Goodnight, Sophia."

"Truth . . . or dare," she taunted like some kind of schoolgirl as I crossed the street at McKinney. Bread Winners Café had been closed for an hour. Loved their buttermilk pan fried chicken breast. After a bunch of airplane pretzel bites, that would've been right on time.

I kept walking.

"Truth or dare," she repeated. Louder this time. Attracted the attention of some of the people as they walked by.

My roller bag stopped on a crack, incomplete in its click-clack across it. "Dare," I called out without looking back to acknowledge her.

"Why? Because the truth is too much? Because somebody's scared? Because you can't handle the truth?" she teased.

"I said dare. That's how the game goes. No questions. Now . . . proceed."

"Okay. I dare you to indulge me a little while longer, *Chris*," she said, finally overtaking me. "It's the least you could do."

"Okay," I indulged. "Truth or dare?"

"Truth," she answered as she took my hand, placing it on her chest so I could feel her heartbeat.

"What's your ex's name?"

"Ivan. Why?"

"You said I made you cum harder than him. Did I make you cum harder than Natalia?" I asked, paying extra close attention to her heartbeat.

"It's different with a woman. Don't know what else to tell you." She shrugged. "Truth or dare?"

"Dare."

She sighed, realizing I would never answer any other way. "I dare you to let me in."

The muscles in my neck constricted as I tightened my grip on my bag handle. "How?"

"It can't end here. Not just yet. Let me spend the night with you."

I took a deep breath then led her down McKinney to my apartment.

Reckless. Foolish. Stupid.

I did say dare, after all.

Chapter 20

Sophia's bag rested at the door where I left it. A black wheeled reminder that her time here was fleeting. I led her to my sofa, skipping the guided tour. The place was sparsely furnished anyway. Minimalist contemporary allowed me to pack up and go at a moment's notice, without fear of someone going through my shit. Most of my secrets dwelled in my head and on my laptop that I'd placed on the small table in front of my window view.

As I got her a glass of water from the kitchen, I could hear it: A faint seductive melody, barely noticeable as it called to me. But it was there if you knew to listen for it. I told myself it was just the pussy and not the person.

"This is a nice place," she proclaimed as I turned on the tap.

"Thanks," I replied as I stuck my finger into the cool running water, splitting the stream. When she thought no one was looking, my mother would wash her hands constantly, some attempt on a deeper level to rid herself of whatever stained her so. *Out, damned spot*, indeed. Some real Macbeth shit.

It was said in ancient times that the gods spoke to mere mortals through running water, rivers and such. I listened for similar guidance, courtesy of the DWU, Dallas Water Utilities.

When I returned with the glass of cold water, her legs were apart, waiting for me to bridge the gap. Perhaps the water was meant to douse the burning flame that existed there. She drank it instead. In her other hand, she held open my copy of Sun Tzu's *The Art of War*. She'd snuck over to my bookshelf that quick.

"Figured you'd have something like this for reading material," she scoffed. "But what's up with the mythology stuff? The Iliad? The Odyssey?"

"You'd be surprised at what you learn. Both real and imagined," I answered. I appreciated that she hadn't chose to examine those particular books more closely. I sat in the chair, across the coffee table from her. A safe zone.

"Is everything about war or a struggle of some sort?"

"Yes."

"Is that what you felt about me and Natalia back in Vegas? Like you're competing with her for me on some level?"

I chuckled. The woman was trying to psychoanalyze a psycho. Kudos to her. "Maybe," I answered.

"Want to compete with her?" she asked as she placed her empty glass on the coffee table. She wiped the excess water from the edge of her sexy mouth. "You can start here."

The whispers became screams as she spread her legs further.

I stepped over the table. Got down on my knees and placed my head under her dress, ignoring any reason and wisdom I'd learned from the water gods of the kitchen sink.

I began at her knees, lathering the insides of her powerful thighs with tiny wet kisses. The closer I got to her gooey center, the more labored her breathing became. I nuzzled my tongue against her clit, savoring her damp, deep heat. She moaned sweetly. Perfectly. She was already so wet. I went deeper, in search of more. Eating, tasting, and partaking of her power.

Determined to break her bewitching spell over me by breaking her instead.

To her, I probably appeared weak.

Good. *Appear strong when you are weak. Weak when you are strong.* Sun Tzu.

"Mmm. That's it. Eat it, Truth. Eat that pussy right," she urged, giddy with pleasure as she rocked back and forth on the sofa. Her legs opened and closed around my head like a taco shell.

Instincts guided me, even as I did something against the better of them. I paused from my feast, needing to clear my head for a sec.

"What? What's wrong?" she murmured.

I didn't answer. Just ripped her dress off instead, eliciting gasps with each harsh yank. She lay bare before me as I stood up. She was so beautiful. An angel with wings made of lies.

She smirked, toying with her hair as she invited me to do more than just gaze.

Beautiful and devious.

I scooped her up and carried her to my bedroom. She bit on my neck again as I held her in my arms, cradling her warm body next to me.

"You're going to make me drop you," I teased as she sucked harder, determined to leave a mark.

"You wouldn't dare," she said as she paused from my neck.

I startled her by relinquishing my hold. Rather than hitting the floor, as she'd anticipated, she landed softly atop my mattress.

"Oops."

"You asshole," she joked as I undressed. When I was done, I watched her watching me. Her eyes narrowed on my dick. "Mmm. I've wanted some more of that since we were on the plane."

I joined her on the bed, inching closer. As our bodies began to touch, she stuck up her hand to stop me.

"Truth or dare?" she asked, delicately this time. Seemed almost fragile.

"Truth."

"Are you going to fuck me or make love to me?"

"Make love to you," I replied as I looked into her eyes.

In my bed, which I shared with no one, I fucked her.

A rattle in my apartment woke me. I'd forgotten Sophia was still there. Looking around my room, I saw the wrinkled sheets gathered by my feet. Condom wrappers lay discarded across the bed and on the floor. Amidst the latex, essence of our union still permeated the atmosphere. While exhaustion was to be expected, the pounding headache that accompanied it wasn't. I looked at the clock.

Five hours I'd been asleep.

That many hours at one time was a rarity for me. Rare enough that it raised concerns. The glass of water that Sophia had gotten me in the middle of our session was gone from the nightstand. I rubbed my eyes then quietly forced myself out of bed, restraining a grunt as I stood.

Other than debris from the damage we wrought, the bedroom looked the same. She hadn't stolen my wallet, thank God. I walked to my closet, checking the variety of clothes, accessories, and disguises I used before removing the air vent to retrieve something.

"Thought you'd never wake up," Sophia said when I staggered out of the bedroom. She had changed into something from her suitcase. Unlike me, she looked fit, as if ready for one of her jogs. She sat near my laptop, but it was still shut. She'd resumed her reading of *The Art of War*, but had turned on the TV, keeping the volume low. "I just can't get enough of those two," she joked.

On the fifty-two-inch screen, CNN was covering the music awards that would be airing that night from Las Vegas. Penny Antnee and Natalia were having a major PDA for the media, deciding to fully acknowledge their relationship, as well a possible reality show in the works. The reporter was asking them something during the pre-show, while Natalia cut sweet eyes at her boo. I didn't waste much time on the scripted fantasy, as I was too busy looking for something awry in my place.

"Nothing to say after last night, lover?"

"Just that my head is killing me," I replied. "What'd you do with my glass of water I had at bedside?"

"I spilled the rest when I got up, so I put it in the dishwasher. Want me to make you some breakfast?" she asked as she sprang up from the chair, offering no hint as to whether she'd drugged me. "I have to warn you, I'm not the best cook."

I interrupted her, placing the bundle of rubber band–bound cash in her hand instead.

"You said ten K for Vegas. What's the extra loot for? I hope you don't think—"

"No, I don't think," I replied, referring to what had gone down between us. "I just need you to go."

"Need some time to yourself?"

"No. I need you to leave town. Tell Collette whatever you think she'll believe. That money there should get you established and back on your feet . . . wherever you choose to go."

"Uh-huh," she hissed. "As long as it's not around here."

Sophia slapped me. Leveled a strike that watered my eyes and added to the intense pounding in my skull. For someone as light as she was, she had a lot of power behind her open hand.

"Knew you were smart," I said, turning my back to shuffle off to my bedroom without acknowledging the internal hurt she felt, nor the hurt my face felt.

"You're in love."

"Excuse me?"

"Not with me though. Unh-uh. I'm not good enough for you," she said, scowl evident. "It's Collette. You want her all to yourself."

"No, but she needs protecting. You're bad for her."

"And you're so good? You are a twisted motherfucker, Truth."

"Don't call me that. Ever again."

"I don't appreciate being threatened."

"You're not. You've been paid. Well. Do you have a problem with my money?"

Sophia ran her thumb over the edges of the bills. "No," she mumbled, defeated. "No problem."

"Then see yourself out."

"Even bad people who do evil things need love, *Chris*. Mark my words: You'll come to realize that one day," she spat just before wheeling her suitcase out the door.

People also need trust, something I could never have with Sophia. Depending on one's perspective, she was either too good, or too bad, to keep around.

I reached for my phone, taking it with me as I went to my bookshelf. I selected an old book on Greek mythology, cracking the weathered cover for the first time in months. Had to be sure it was still there. While I was sleeping, Sophia could've rifled through everything.

"Yes, this is Mr. Davis. I'd like to switch units. Preferably on another floor," I said to the building manager when she answered. As she attempted to fathom my request, I reread the clipping stowed in my book. It was from the *Times Picayune* back in New Orleans. Something I held onto. The article told the flowery tragic tale of a failed soap star who hurled herself off the Mississippi River Bridge one day. It claimed the depressed suicidal woman had no children, and nobody left behind, other than her estranged brother. A lawyer. Jason had told me something about my not having a birth certificate, having never attended school, and the issue of not knowing my father might complicate things. I was just a complication to him. A complication and a tool.

Outside my apartment window, it was a perfect day.

"Why?" I asked, echoing the manager's inquiry. "Because I'm not pleased with the view."

Chapter 21

I entered the bookstore, playing the role of the happy sap; pretending as if none of the past week had occurred between Sophia and me.

I skipped the hated coffee blend this time, naturally anxious and excited to see her. She sat in what was my regular spot for these meetings, unnerving me. Facing me, as if she were on the lookout for my arrival.

But that was impossible.

"Hey," I said, ignoring her change of seats as I planted a friendly kiss on her cheek. It wasn't something I would normally do, but I was genuinely pleased that she was here.

"Somebody's in a good mood," she responded, a rare funkiness evident in her tone. "Skipped the coffee?"

"Yeah . . . how did—" I gasped before realizing the obvious. Those damn senses of hers. "You did too?" I asked, noticing her missing cup, but with the more traditional sense.

"Yes. I wasn't in the mood for a pick-me-up."

"Somebody's in a bad mood," I quipped as I claimed the seat she normally held.

"So observant," she taunted. "I guess that's why you're a writer. Speaking of that, how's the story coming along?

"Good. Completed a bunch of chapters this weekend. Guess I've been inspired."

"And yet you still refuse to read one to me. A shame."

"Something on your mind, Collette?" I asked, leaning toward her.

"My cousin Sophia left."

"Oh?"

"I kind of enjoyed the company, to tell you the truth. She was a trip."

"Yeah," I agreed. "Saw that much when you introduced us. Where'd she go?"

"Don't know." She sighed. "She went out of town for an interview or something, came back and grabbed her stuff. For someone with a new job, she was pretty salty. Wouldn't even tell me what kind of job or where she was heading. Figured she owed me at least that. When I asked her to check the attitude at the door, we got into it."

"Oh. I'm sorry to hear that."

"Don't be," she said with a smile briefly returning to her delicate features. "You didn't have anything to do with it. I don't like to speak ill of family, but Sophia is a devious person. I'm just one of the rare relatives that indulge her."

"I had no idea."

"You wouldn't. She can be a charmer."

"Not that it's any of my business," I prefaced, "but do you think she's involved in something shady?"

"I hope not," she replied with a sigh at the end. "But I don't want to talk about that anymore. I've missed you, Chris."

Now I smiled. Felt genuine warmth. I stood up, came over. Allowed her to touch my hand. "Ditto. Want me to get our usual?"

"I think I'd like that now," Collette replied.

I held up my hand to signal our usual orders to the barista, but suddenly put it down.

"How about something different for a change?" I asked, turning my attention back to Collette.

"What do you suggest?"

"Bread Winners Café," I replied. "A good meal, good company, and a couple of glasses of wine?"

"What if I'm not hungry?" she posed.

"Drink the wine."

She smiled, more broadly this time.

Chapter 22

Three Years Ago

I was parked on Eads Street, sitting alone in the dark. Scarface's lyrics to "I Seen a Man Die" had me in an introspective mood as I watched the house. While others were struggling through finals, I was concentrating on my master's thesis. This was one of my first jobs free of Jason's reigns. A young man going solo, feeling his way in the world. I didn't have to be here, but I wanted to.

One of those "If a tree falls in the forest and no one's there to hear it . . ." situations. Had what I planned really brought things to this moment?

The doctor returned to his restored Oak Cliff home an hour ago, having rushed inside after leaving his office early.

His name?

Not important.

The home was a piece of history, built in the early 1900s. He and his wife bought it a little over two years ago for around half a million.

His mistress paid me forty thousand, a down payment of a sort on her own future home. A home with the doctor—except he was never leaving his precious wife for her. No matter how exquisite the head she gave him. No matter how well they cliqued. No matter how much of himself he shared. There was a part she would never possess.

She knew that, but refused to accept it. Her goal was to make his wife no longer so precious; no longer free of taint. Maybe he'd change his mind then.

Desperation with a checkbook had found its instrument in me.

Last week, the doctor had received a few hangup calls to set things up. The hired actor played his part. Brash and physical to the doctor's cool and calculating, he was the perfect foil. He met the doctor today at an outdoor location, telling him where to find the evidence of their trysts inside their home—the used condom and stained panties, false evidence I'd planted when the cable repairman allowed me to accompany him as a helper yesterday.

The doctor would be devastated, but ready to move on when the dust settled. But in addition to being proud, men can be possessive and territorial. Add guilt to that mix, and things can become unpredictable, something neither I nor his mistress had completely factored into this.

In my haste to accept the job, I hadn't spent enough time learning whether the doctor was prone to violence. Sloppy. For all I knew, he could be waiting with a butcher knife.

I was being silly. The man had a professional career to think about.

Her Audi TT arrived, parking in front of the house as its headlights went out. Nothing stirred inside the home. No lights came on that I could see. From her tiny trunk, his wife removed two small grocery bags, probably intent on preparing dinner.

Such devotion and innocence. I almost felt sorry for her. A tinge of guilt crept in, growing the closer she came to the front door.

As she put her key in the door and opened it, I imagine she only saw the faint spark of the cigarette lighter. Probably didn't smell the natural gas just before her world exploded in a cascading inferno of flame and exploding glass, and his world ended.

Fini.

The explosion shook the block, setting off car alarms. I saw her on the ground amidst the smoldering debris, her blouse afire as she rolled around, writhing in pain.

Before my mind had registered it, I was sprinting down the street.

All I heard were her screams as I pulled her to safety, swatting out the fire on her clothing as we went.

"It's going to be all right," I repeated, a mantra more for me than her. She didn't listen, just kept screaming as she kept her hands cupped to her face.

When I managed to move her hands away, I realized how wrong I was.

Her frantic sobs were haunting.

Her eyes.

"Oh my God," I muttered as I witnessed her by the light of the burning structure.

She had shrapnel in her eyes.

Collette was her name.

Chapter 23

One month ago . . . Dallas

We were at the game in Irving. The final season in the old stadium. Perfect timing for them to come to town.

We greeted them with boos, as we should, the roar and rush of a crowd reviling these black-and-silver pirates intent on stealing a win from The Boys.

On all the beer, hot dogs, and Dr. Pepper in the place, that wasn't going to happen.

I marveled at how her senses handled everything, how she kept from being overwhelmed by all the voices, sounds, and smells. She held my hand tightly, as if she knew I was curious, and wanted to convey those sensations and what she was experiencing to me.

"Having a good time?" I asked.

"Totally," she replied with as warm a smile as I'd ever seen grace her beautiful face. "I haven't done this since . . ."

"Since some other guy asked you out to a football game?" I clumsily joked.

She swung her free hand, managing to land a fist on my shoulder. "I'm trying to enjoy things and you keep coming with the jokes. What's the score?" she asked.

"Twenty-one to six," I answered.

"We're winning, right?"

"Can't you tell from the crowd?"

In spite of the expected ass-whipping, something was off with Oakland's performance. I turned my binoculars toward the field, curious as to how large my role might be in it all. Andre Martin, Oakland's star wide receiver, fumbled the ball on what was a sure touchdown pass. The home crowd whipped up into another frenzy of cheers and laughs. When the Dallas player said something to him about it, Andre blew up and shoved him. The referee called a penalty for his extra effort. When he kept yapping, another personal foul was tossed on.

For a man who had grown into a marketable role model recently, Andre was certainly regressing. Team chemistry in disarray and a meltdown on display. When he got to the sideline, Oakland's coach told Andre, in not so nice terms, to take the bench. Any chance of Oakland at least making the game respectable was slip-sliding away.

On Dallas's next possession, they threw an interception, a result of the football bouncing into the air when it struck someone's helmet. Oakland was fading, but still had a shot. Rather than putting Andre in to redeem himself, the coach turned to San Antonio Jackson.

In Las Vegas, San Antonio said he wanted to ruin Andre's life, take away what Andre *thought* he had. San Antonio was showing just how determined he was to make that a reality.

"Touchdown, Oakland," the announcer delivered as San Antonio celebrated another eviscerating swipe across Andre's wounded psyche. I wondered how news of the photos had been presented to him. If San Antonio were really out for revenge, he probably leaked word about Andre to their teammates. Death by tiny cuts, as they all reassessed their relationships with their once-rising star.

Andre had a towel draped over his head, ignoring the celebratory atmosphere. I smirked, continuing to watch as San Antonio played for the network cameras. The man was a good actor. He came over by the bench, where the lone Andre dwelled, placing his hand on his shoulder like the big brother he used to be.

Before Andre's betrayal.

Before San Antonio sought me out to deal with that betrayal.

When San Antonio tried to talk to Andre, Andre attacked him, shoving San Antonio into a Gatorade bucket. To the world, it seemed an ungrateful, jealous teammate was biting the hand that fed him. It had to bring San Antonio some level of satisfaction at this point.

"You're being too quiet, Chris. What am I missing?" Collette asked.

"Just the end of the game," I said as I lowered my binoculars. I placed her hand on my bicep, resting my hand atop hers to lead her from the stadium.

We shared a light dinner before returning to her apartment. After dinner, she was up for company and asked if I'd stay awhile. Of course, I obliged. As reluctant as I was to admit it, there was nothing I wouldn't do for her. Her dimly lit place was earthier than mine—rich colors and textures, from deep burgundy walls to imported bamboo table lamps, provided an intimacy that exuded warmth and class. The strategically placed potted ferns showed evidence of the love that had been given to them. All from someone who relied on memories past, of a hidden sight.

Made me ashamed of my spartan existence, the empty vessel I was. Maybe that's what I wanted . . . needed from her: someone to make me feel something.

I imagined that everything in here was fixed, set according to a system that allowed Collette to live a normal life. I feared moving anything out of place, but curiously eyed her reading material. Several James Patterson novels—of course, both in Braille and audio—sat in a convenient location next to a CD on erotic massage techniques. I smiled to myself at that one, knowing how expressive she could be with her hands in the most mundane of situations. My mind wandering in a devious direction, I almost missed the other Patterson work. It was a regular print edition. Basic worn, printed words with nothing spectacular to it—except for the burn marks on the margins and secondary smell of smoke when I put it to my nose.

Apparently, she and Patterson went back much longer than she and I. Advantage: the real author.

I heard the rushing water as Collette showered. Down the darkened hall, I could just make out the railing installed along the wall. Rather than enter the abyss in search of her, I sat back down, turning on the TV to pass the time. ESPN News had highlights from the Oakland/Dallas game that evening. In particular, the sideline fight, which

was the tantalizing side story to Oakland's loss. I
fished my laptop from my backpack on the side of
the sofa. Opening it, I sent digital photos of Andre
Martin to the website 4Shizzle—the same ones I'd
given to San Antonio Jackson back in Vegas, timing this to further his purposes and reinforce the
negative buzz he wanted.

*Wakey. Wakey. Someone's got a present for
you,* I casually typed as the dialogue box opened
between me and my paying customer.

> *And it's not even Christmas. You "sound"
> like you're in a good mood.*

*What can I say? Things are good. Life is good.
You must be getting some. Trying to make me
jealous. Let me look at what you sent.*

I waited while she uploaded the images somewhere on the East Coast. Allowed her to digest
what the pixels told her.

> *Who's that?*
> *Andre Martin. Heard of him?* I asked
> sarcastically.
> *Damn. Didn't recognize bottom boy with
> his face all contorted. Hurts so good, I guess.*
> *The other pic is of more suitable quality.*
> *This is some heavy shit. Wasn't he just
> on ESPN actin' the ass?*

IDK.

Think this had anything to do with his stank attitude in the game?

IDK. I'm just a nobody sending u pictures.

U are SO full of shit. Who's the muscle-bound so-and-so putting the lumber to him?

Not important, I typed.

If it's not important, then why did you obscure him?

She was a quick one. Like Jason.

Because you're not paying me for that, I replied.

How can you be sure I'm paying you for this anyway? Might be photoshopped.

U know better.

Not so cheerful now, huh? Can't even make out the tats on the man's arm, the anonymous cyber-editor complained. *I smell a bigger story. If I offer more $$$, would you consider giving me the unedited pics?*

Not yet . . . at least.

Collette returned, fresh from her shower. "What are you doing?" she asked as she felt for the arm of the sofa. I resisted the urge to help, having been scolded by her too often.

"Checking the news and outlining the next chapter," I replied. She had to have heard my keystrokes. No point in being totally dishonest.

Are you there?
Gotta run.
I'll let you hit it then quit it this time, but don't get used to it.
LOL. Funny. Will be in touch.

Collette sat next to me, smelling of sweet oils and gardenia, her curly hair wet from the shower. She rested snugly in her soft cotton robe. I abruptly ended my online talk, feeling guilty about the lurid images that I'd just shared. Made me think of her cousin Sophia for the briefest of moments. But she was long gone from the equation; everything in balance now with the absence of that random variable.

"You promised," she complained, acknowledging the faint whir of my laptop's cooling fan. "Do you ever stop working?"

"Sorry. It's a bad habit of mine, but pays the bills."

"What's it . . . about?" she asked, kissing my ear ever so subtly, her irritation subsided. Made me wonder what else she'd been doing while in the shower. In spite of my desires, rushing was not something I wanted to do with Collette. Slow and easy had been my way since this courtship began months ago.

"I'm not . . . supposed to tell you. Remember?"

"Just this once. Please, Chris. Share something of yourself with me. I've never been able to ask this of a real writer before."

"Okay. It's about a bad man who does bad things," I relented, closing my eyes as Collette sucked on my neck. It was so soft, so subtle that I almost didn't feel it until she'd been well on her way.

"Does he pay the price in the end?" she whispered, pausing from her groove.

"I don't know yet. It's too early in the book," I replied as my pulse sped. It was hard lying to her about what was a blank screen with no story on it.

"Maybe he finds redemption."

Not meaning to, I laughed. Killed the vibe dead. "That's how you want it to end?" I asked.

"I suppose. But it's not my story to tell."

"It could be. Want me to write it that way for you?"

"No. Then it wouldn't be yours. And I don't want you to do something just for me. James Patterson wouldn't."

"That's just it. I'm no Patterson. You should have someone doing something just for you. You're special, Collette. Special to me. And I would write the story that way if you want me to. I mean it."

She sighed, taking my hand in hers and rubbing it vigorously. "Y'know, it's been too long since someone's treated me like this. Thank you."

"You're welcome," I replied before kissing her on the forehead. "Are you ever going to tell me what happened . . . with . . . ?"

"Now?" Although absent of sight, she knew where my eyes were focused.

"If it still bothers you, you don't have to." My voice wavered, too pushy in my attempt at intimacy. Images of that night ran through my mind as, absent her dark shades, I noticed the faint physical scars that remained. This was her home. No need to wear them.

"It doesn't. It's just that I'm not sure myself. Still," she replied. She smiled, albeit a nervous one. "One day, my husband did something completely out of character and it resulted in this. I suppose I never really knew him."

"Probably vice versa. He didn't know you. Or how special you really are."

Collette giggled nervously. "You knew Myron?" she joked, grazing the truth in her ignorance.

"That's his name?" James. His middle name was James. Graduated third from the top of his class in medical school.

"*Was* his name."

"Oh. I'm sorry about having you relive—"

"Stop," she interrupted. "Just stop. I don't want any sadness or regret spoiling our day, Chris. Do you understand me?"

"Yes, ma'am," I said with a laugh. She took her bare foot, sidling it comfortably beneath the bend of my leg. I gently ran my hand across her leg, massaging her calf. Things grew quiet as I turned off her television, allowing me to hear the soft moan escaping her lips.

"Chris?" she called out as I moved my hand up her thigh.

"Yes?"

"What are we doing?"

"Living," I replied, sensing the tremors building within her as I rubbed her clit.

"Loving?"

"Yes."

"I . . . I want you," she said.

I lifted Collette from the sofa, carrying her in my arms as if she were precious cargo. As we entered the abyss of her hallway, I left the lights off. Light wasn't needed, for I held my torch to keep the darkness at bay.

Chapter 24

"Yeah. Yeah. I can come by tonight. I miss you too," I replied as I paced on my balcony. I had accepted another job and was strategizing in my head while talking to Collette—contemplating someone's ruination while I basked in the glow of my newfound happiness.

This job wasn't as bad as others.

Simple blackmail. A regular private detective would suffice, but I guess they wanted to be *exotic*. Something I could arrange over the phone with minimum effort.

Nothing as complicated as the Vegas job for Ja—

"Collette, let me call you back," I said as I shoved the sliding glass door aside to run back in.

Whatever was on the news hadn't piqued my interest until the very end.

I know I didn't imagine it. I knew her face well enough. It was that singer Natalia.

Careful not to change channels, I rewound the news program on the DVR back to the beginning of the story.

Multiple shootings.

It was a bloody day in Houston, ending in three dead and one in critical condition. Something about an audition where a singer had been shot.

The singer wasn't Natalia though; rather someone she had some connection to. A former contestant of that reality show *U.S. Icon;* that much was clear when the cameras switched to a visibly shaken Natalia as she arrived at the hospital.

"No comment," she said as she rushed by the throngs of cameras and boom mikes.

A singer near death.

And connected to Natalia.

This had Jason's fingerprints all over it.

And maybe mine, in some manner. Unforeseen consequences.

Shit.

I scrolled through the numbers on my cell, selecting the appropriate one. The one I knew he'd pick up.

"We need to talk," I said when Jason answered.

***

We agreed to meet in the Continental Presidents Club lounge at Terminal One of the Fort Lauderdale airport. Jason had somewhere to be, but I demanded this, since he refused to discuss anything over the phone. Besides, it was easier to tell if he was lying to my face. Made the last minute flight worth it.

"You came as yourself, Truth. How nice," Jason remarked as I approached his table. Only two bodyguards flanked him this time. New ones. Deadly professionals, by their look. A sure sign that he was moving up. Jason looked at his watch, anticipating his flight back to Houston, where On-Phire had recently set up shop. Better for him to have been absent when everything went to hell, I thought, as it gave him plausible deniability. "Make it fast. I'm in a foul mood."

"Somebody didn't give you enough hugs?" I joked. Neither of his sentries reacted.

"You're not funny, dear boy. And I hate wasting time and resources, so it's good that you came."

"I called you. Remember?"

"Whatever. I have a job for you."

"Clean up on aisle one back in Houston?" Jason's eye twitched, his body betraying that he had some role in those shootings. "No thanks."

"If you're not going to help me, then why come out here, nephew? Maybe *you* need a hug," he shot back. "Oh, that's right. You're finally getting those. Plan on making Dallas your permanent home? Your mother would be so proud. But whatever happened to that beguiling young thing you had on your arm back in Vegas? She learned too much about you?"

I denied him the satisfaction of seeing how his remarks really affected me. "Careful. Family only gets you so much leeway," I said. "I just wanted to ask you if the fireworks in H-town have anything to do with the Natalia stuff we participated in."

Jason motioned for his thugs to give us some more space. When they did, he gestured for me to take a seat. I indulged him, knowing he had a flight to catch.

"What if they did?"

"Then I'm done. Looked like some out of control shit you set in motion. I don't want to know what it's about, but some of those people had to be innocents."

"Hey, you've been doing this for me long enough. To make an omelet, you have to break some eggs. Thing is, after putting in a lot of money and patience, I'm left with nothing but crap."

"I have my limits, Jason."

"You mean since you fucked up that time?" he asked, throwing my miscalculation with Collette in my face as if it were a pot of scalding water. "That wasn't one of my jobs anyway. You were freelancing that time, remember? And look where it got you." He *tsk*ed.

"Don't go there. Don't you fuckin' go there," I snarled, jabbing my finger toward him in a way that drew the attention of both bodyguards. Jason nodded at them, indicating no threat.

"Truth, I know we don't have the most cordial relationship, but you're family. And you are gifted," he said, checking his watch before he stood up. It was time to go. "That allows me to overlook that mouth on you and all the disrespectful filth that comes out of it."

"Jason, I mean it. I'm done with you."

"Want to think about it?"

"Nope," I replied, not bothering to get up. "Enjoy your flight. Consider this our good-bye."

"You need allies in this world, dear boy. Do you really want to be on the other side when it's game time?"

"Just remember, I got your playbook. I know all your tricks and secrets. Something to think about if you ever consider taking the field against me."

"Good night, Truth," Jason said as he left the lounge with an eerie calmness that I did not know how to read.

I wasn't left alone long before my phone rang.

"Hello?" I answered.

"Chris, where are you?" Collette asked. "I thought you were coming by."

"Oh," I said, slapping my forehead. "I'm so sorry. An emergency came up."

"Is everything all right?"

"It will be now," I said with a smile, forcing myself to believe it. My flight back to Dallas would be boarding within the hour.

Chapter 25

Collette screamed, waving her hands in the air as we drifted sideways on our descent. I gunned the accelerator, a violent but thrilling exercise as I guided the wheel to control our rollercoaster spiral down the parking garage exit ramp. With the top down, we could hear the engine revs reverberating off the walls, could smell the burnt rubber of the tires.

"You are crazy!" she shouted as she braced herself again in her seat. Try as she might to avoid it, a smile escaped.

The Audi TT, while being a roadster, was close enough to the one she dearly remembered. When she could drive. I bought this one as a reminder of those happier times. Despite transactions like this attracting unwanted attention, it was a bit of fun for me as well.

I'd become too comfortable as Chris, my answers and responses to Collette now second nature. The layers I hid behind were becoming as comfortable as a worn pair of jeans. The lovely lady at my side made me feel things I'd rarely confronted. Even had me entertaining something as silly as actually writing a novel.

At the bottom of the parking garage, I paid the attendant then exited onto Commerce Street. Like some nervous school kid, I'd brought her to The French Room at the Adolphus Hotel, hoping to impress her with my knowledge of fine dining. But Collette didn't need such things. My company was enough for her.

"This reminds me so much of my old car," Collette offered as we stopped at the corner of Commerce and North Griffin. Her delicate fingers traced over the hills and valleys of the dash, stopping at the Audi symbol. Her mind was in another time. Another car. Another life.

A life I'd abruptly ended.

Maybe the car was a miscalculation on my part, some sick part of me wanting to step in and assume the life, however imperfect, that she and her husband had shared. Or was it a sadistic streak? My innate need to push buttons, as if she were a test subject with which to perfect my methods? No. That couldn't be it. I loved her.

I looked in the rearview mirror. Traffic was light. "Want to drive?" I offered.

She grimaced, turning into the sound of my voice. "That's not even funny," she replied.

"I mean it," I said, putting the car in park and the emergency flashers on. "I trust you completely. I trust you with my life."

"You are crazy, Chris. Completely off your rocker."

"C'mon," I prodded. "Just down the street. We're not that far from your place. I'll even help you steer if you want."

I hit the button to unlock my door, but Collette stopped me before I could exit. She reached out for me, putting her hand in mine. It was trembling.

"Stop. I appreciate what you're doing, but just take me home. Okay?"

"You're pissed," I remarked softly. I was trying too hard. Too much. Too soon.

"No." She chuckled, turning away so I wouldn't see the obvious tears or hear the tightness in her throat. "Just the opposite."

"What?"

"You remind me of better times. I mean, I'm okay with the way things are now, but you are someone I should've known earlier. Before Myron. Before this happened."

"Better late than never, lady. And there's no question as to how I feel about you," I said as I touched her cheek, turning her to face me again. I kissed her tears away, allowing the passion to build and flow between us.

"Get a fuckin' room!" somebody in a tricked-out yellow Civic yelled as it swerved around us. Our interlude interrupted and chemistry rendered inert, we both laughed.

"Let's get you home," I said as I turned off the emergency flashers and rolled out. Before I turned onto North Griffin, I noticed a car that had been behind us. It was pulled over a block back with its headlights out. When I made a move, so did the dark sedan. Paranoia being more lover than friend, perhaps, but I couldn't risk it.

Not with Collette.

We took North Griffin and passed under the Woodall Rodgers Freeway, my eyes still affixed on the rearview mirror as the car hummed along. "Mirror" by Supreme Beings of Leisure played on the stereo courtesy of Collette, who'd turned me on to them. And as she'd turned me on to them, so had she turned me on to her, my stylish, sexy, uncompromising, unusual lady. Rather than continue to McKinney, where my route would've taken us past my place, I made a quick U-turn then switched over to North Field. I accelerated quickly onto Ross Avenue, taking a left, where it would take me to Highway 75.

"Slow down," Collette said as a gust of wind blew across her face. "I know you can drive, so you can stop showing off."

"I'll never stop trying to impress you, lady," I teased.

"Boy, you had me at 'hello,'" she teased back. A shame her introduction was different from mine.

We jumped on Highway 75, passing Griggs Park and the cemetery before taking the third exit at Lemmon Avenue. I stopped short, a block from Collette's place, still unsure if dropping her off was the right thing to do.

"Are we here?" she asked, reaching for the white cane at her side.

"No. For a new car, the top is acting crazy. I'm going to see if I can get it unstuck. Just sit tight."

As I pretended to fumble with the unbroken top, I surveyed my surroundings, looking for the menacing sedan I'd seen earlier, or anything else not quite right.

"You got it?"

"Almost," I answered.

I saw nothing, but just couldn't risk us being followed or watched. Before I returned to the car, my phone rang. I snatched it up, quickly checking the number.

Las Vegas.

No business tonight. I'd call back another time.

Jumping back into the driver's seat, I tried raising the power folding top again. *Somehow* it worked correctly this time.

On the move again, Collette noticed something wasn't right.

"I thought we were near my place," she commented as she found the volume control on the radio and lowered it.

"We are. But I can't take you home," I replied as we sped away.

Chapter 26

I brought Collette to the Gaylord Texan hotel in Grapevine, far away from Uptown, as a means of overcoming my immediate paranoia. It took a great deal of coaxing along the way to convince her to keep our night going. She relented eventually, chalking it up to my wild and crazy nature. Better safe than sorry, I'd learned.

The people in the Civic did say to get a room, after all.

"You never told me you were a kidnapper," Collette remarked as we walked through the gigantic enclosed atrium after checking in. The tapping of her cane on the tiny cobblestones was amplified, as was everything else in the gorgeous closed environment, several square miles in scope. The gentle gurgle of the waterways that flowed through this place was relaxing. Made it feel like a "mini-Disney" escape.

"I'd like to think a kidnapper with taste . . . and an imagination. Besides, that's what you get for picking up strangers in book stores," I said as we passed the few hotel guests and conventioneers exploring the indoor gardens, recreated historic architecture, and restaurants that were still open. Straight ahead lay the elevators to take us to a suite in the Lone Star Tower overlooking everything. Not only romantic, but a good vantage point for me.

My phone rang again. This time, Collette heard it.

Same caller as before. Vegas. Forwarded from one of my other phones.

"Aren't you going to answer it?" she asked, probably noticing the change in my step as I looked at the caller ID.

"It can wait. Trust me."

"Sounds like another woman," she said, grasping correctly, although this particular woman was strictly business as far as I was concerned.

"No," I lied. "Just a headache. And I declared tonight a headache free zone before I picked you up. You're my aspirin, babe."

"You expect me to believe that call wasn't from another woman? Being blind doesn't make me stupid, Chris." She was more playful than combative. A grown-ass woman who was solid to her core.

"I know. And I don't take you for a fool. I wouldn't have gone there with you after all this time if there were some doubts, Collette. You're the only woman for me. The *only* one in my life. No shit."

"Let me see," she said, placing her fingers on my neck to feel my pulse. She removed them after a few quiet seconds. "Hmm," she pondered quizzically. "I believe you, Chris."

"Good. Now can we go up to the room? My feet hurt."

"That's not all that's going to be hurting when I get through with you," Collette joked before we hurried our pace. Smiling to myself, I took her at her word.

Pushing the elevator button, I read the suite number again on the magnetic key card holder. She toyed with my elbow, running her index finger around and around, as though the tiny lines and cracks were a maze. Electricity danced between us, making me warm to my core.

"Anybody around us?" she whispered while we waited on the elevator to arrive.

"Nope. Just me and you," I answered, perking up at her tone. The embers already burning, she ignited me by pulling me closer and engaging me wholeheartedly with deep, full kisses.

Upon its arrival, we entered the elevator. Collette pulled sharply on my shirt, intent on tearing down all barriers between us. As my buttons popped loose, she pulled my white T-shirt from out of my pants. Sliding her hands underneath, she vigorously rubbed my chest and caressed my neck. When her fingers traced my lips, I welcomed them in my mouth, cherishing each tip as though it were the sweetest thing known to man.

"Damn, you make me so horny," she gushed as I continued to suck on her fingers. She dug her face into my chest and kissed with abandon, her warm, damp breath tickling my nipples with every deep gasp.

My breathing becoming more labored, I dug one hand into her curly hair and clutched her ass with the other one, yanking her into me. It took all my control to not rip off her dress and fuck her right there.

Upon reaching our floor, I rushed Collette down the hallway, counting down the rooms as we got closer. With each room number I recited, her anticipation rose. It was as if they were an incantation, the power of numbers working their spell over body and soul.

"Are we there yet?" she asked as we stopped in front of the room.

I didn't answer, instead allowing the click of the lock to alert her. I took her by the hand, leading her into the suite. The room was cool, darkened by the pulled curtains to the balcony. We walked over to the large, plush bed that greeted us.

She exhaled deeply as I unzipped the back of her dress. I glided my hands across her soft shoulders to part the fabric, allowing it to fall to her feet. As she stood there in nothing but a bra and panties, I lazily dragged my tongue from her neck down to the small of her back. I stopped at the tip of her ass crack, softly kissing where the black lace barely obscured the curve of her hips.

"Mmmm," she murmured, her ass flinching and legs quivering as I reached up, undoing the clasp on her bra, which she removed. Stepping out of the crumpled dress around her ankles, she gently backed herself onto the bed. I watched her slide her panties off, hooking them on her heels before kicking them free. As she lay there, I hesitated, torn over what I wanted at this moment and what would be best for Collette. Cold and impersonal was my way. I couldn't front though. She wasn't just a piece of ass. I cared for her. I needed her like a kite does the stiff breeze.

"Come here," she urged, sensing my reluctance. She was so lovely—a mass of femininity exuding equal parts sensuality and sensitivity.

And she wanted me.

Me.

To her, I was someone named Chris. But I knew it was the person inside with which she'd connected.

Me.

Whoever that was.

I removed my clothes and joined her, the contact with her skin intoxicating as we writhed in unison atop the thick comforter. Collette squirmed, excited by the passionate kisses I lavished upon her stomach and on her breasts. As I slid atop her, she ran her fingers through my hair, pulling me closer for a kiss. Her tongue was tasty as I took it in my mouth. Entrapping me between her legs, her hands went to places she'd probably wanted to go, but was reluctant to admit.

She gasped when she felt my swollen dick.

"Damn," she grunted. Catching how she sounded, she giggled. "Sorry."

"It's okay," I replied, looking at her and seeing the delight on her face. She began stroking me, eliciting a deep growl from me the harder she worked. Hands of magic. Before long she'd have me howling at the moon.

"Do you have any condoms?" she asked, slowing in her coaxing of me. Allowed me to get control of myself. That phone call obviously had mistrust on her mind, no matter what she said.

"Yeah," I answered, looking for my pants in the darkened room. As I fetched them from the floor, I noticed Collette running her hands over her body in a slow, deliberate manner. As if checking how she looked for me. No need. She was perfect.

"Are you sure you want to tonight?" I asked, considering what originally set us on this path.

Collette didn't speak of it, and I wasn't supposed to know, but tonight was their anniversary. Her husband, although a cheating piece of shit, was supposed to be here instead. And she wasn't supposed to be . . .

"You don't want to?" she asked, her voice faltering.

"I didn't say that," I replied as I tore back the foil wrapper.

My phone rang again, but I was too busy making love to Collette. On her anniversary.

Chapter 27

"Got a reason for blowing up my phone?" I queried after putting on my boxers and quietly slipping onto the balcony. Conventioneers several stories below had gathered in the atrium for a morning buffet while scrolling through their BlackBerries. Collette was still asleep, but I'd already ordered room service. We needed to get our energy back after expending so much on each other.

"Huh? Who dis?" Peaches asked, yawning in return. Bitch was groggy. Figuring the time difference, she'd probably been off work a few hours—or satisfying a late but well-paying customer from The Standard.

"Taylor," I replied low, not knowing just how much I'd rocked Collette's world. She didn't need to know any names for me other than Chris.

"Hmph. Doesn't sound like you," she grunted as I heard her rustling through her sheets to better position herself.

"Got a cold," I replied, realizing I'd slipped up with my accent and cadence, which I quickly rectified. Sloppy. "Now, what the fuck do you want?" I continued.

"I was trying to tell you about them people."

"*People*?"

"Yeah. People been coming around The Standard. Asking what I know."

"About?"

"You."

Sometimes you start to believe your own press clippings: that you can do no wrong, that you're always five steps ahead. The guise Peaches knew could be discarded, but it still bothered me that someone was this close to be asking her about me. "What about me?" I asked further.

"Who you are, where you live, how they can get in touch with you."

"What's that all about?"

"Probably something to do with San Antonio."

"What happened in San Antonio?" I asked, worried that someone had tracked me to the right state, even if the wrong city.

"No," she answered, "San Antonio Jackson. The football player. He was the last dealings I had with you. You heard what happened to him, huh?"

"Of course," I lied without missing a beat. I hadn't heard shit. My laptop, normally at my side, was back at my place, and I hadn't checked the news. I'd been wrapped up in Collette, and had voluntarily cut myself off from the usual resources for a full twenty-four hours.

"I'm scared, baby," Peaches offered. I could tell she truly was. "My uncle owns the club and is keeping them off my back, but I might have to give them something. These motherfuckers ain't the kind to play with. Ya feel me?"

"Yeah, I feel ya," I replied, knowing our relationship was at an end. She'd never see or speak to the man she knew as Taylor again. The phone number she'd used to reach me would be turned off. "You seen them fools around The Standard before?"

"Nah, baby. And I don't want to see them again if I can help it."

"I gotcha. Thanks."

"You're welcome." She sighed. "Anything you want me to do or say . . . if I have to?"

"Nah. Just do you." Through the curtains I thought I saw Collette stirring in the bed. "Take care of yourself, Peaches."

"You too, baby."

I hung up, composing myself before returning to our suite. Maybe putting all of this behind me might be for the best. Become Chris full time for Collette. I had enough money saved up.

Who was I kidding?

Destruction flowed through my veins. Chaos was the crown I proudly wore.

"Good morning," Collette called out while wrapping the sheets around her body. Her hair flowed wild and free, as unrestrained as she'd been in giving herself to me. Made me want to get all up in it again. "Did you return your call?

"Yeah. Didn't want to wake you," I offered, unaware whether she could've heard my conversation . . . or my intent.

She yawned then stretched her trim ebony arms. The sheet slipped away, exposing lovely breasts and erect nipples. "Anything urgent?" she asked, pulling the sheet back up.

"Just a little," I replied as I crawled back into bed. "My agent says my deadline has been moved up."

"And I'm keeping you from your writing?"

"No, not at all," I answered. "You're more inspiration than distraction."

"Silver-tongued devil," Collette joked. "I don't know why I ever doubted you were what you say you are."

"What else would I be? A secret agent? A serial killer? I'm hurt that you doubted me."

"Don't be. It's just my questioning nature. Well, that and your never letting me read any of your books. And I still don't know your pen name."

"How about if I promise to tell you all about this one when I'm finished?"

"I'd like that," she replied, coming in for a friendly peck on the lips.

A knock came at the door. Breakfast was here.

"You surprised me with breakfast too?" Collette guessed.

"Who said I ordered for you?" I teased, to which she playfully shoved me. "Be right back," I said, exiting the bed.

"Your paper, sir," the hotel staff member said with a distinct West African accent when I answered. I took the courtesy copy of *USA Today*, signing the receipt with my other hand, the one opposite my usual, before rolling the loaded cart in myself. I ordered continental for her, with a cup of fresh fruit. Although I'd ordered a heartier choice for myself, I no longer had an appetite, thanks to my conversation with Peaches. The unknown was nagging at me. After placing Collette's tray beside her, I sifted through the paper instead.

"You're not eating?" she asked. Damn, she was too perceptive at times.

"Thinking about work," I answered as I located the story on San Antonio Jackson. He was back home in Cleveland after breaking both his legs in some sort of accident. He'd walk again, but the sports writer was speculating that his career was over, reflecting on what that meant for Oakland as a team moving forward. A cold world we live in.

Despite what was out about Andre Martin, this seemed too vicious for him. For the briefest of moments, I considered who else was in those incriminating photos with Andre.

But no one had the unaltered photos except for me.

"Penny for your thoughts?"

"Huh? *What did you say?*"

Collette chuckled. "Is there something you need to do, silly? You've been 'off' ever since your call."

"It'll wait," I replied, taking a bite of my bacon. "It'll wait."

Chapter 28

I revved the portable blower strapped to my back, guiding the gentle autumn leaves into a pile prior to winter's icy grasp that would soon be claiming these suburbs. The man had a big-ass yard.

San Antonio Jackson sat alone outside in his wheelchair, the bitter cold his form of therapy. Or maybe he didn't want to face the television coverage and ringing telephones inside. His wife left earlier in the limo, leaving him with bodyguards stationed on the grounds of his McMansion. More than just an accident had happened.

I could've left it alone. Nobody could catch me, but I wanted to know who had the balls to try. Having waited over an hour in the cold, hanging with the lawn crew, I came closer, chasing a renegade leaf all the way to San Antonio's back deck.

"Hey! Hey! Could you blow that thing somewhere else?" he yelled. I was close enough to see a black eye too.

"Sir?" I replied, easing off the throttle.

"I'm trying to relax, my man. Can you come back tomorrow?"

I stepped up partially onto his deck, taking off my work gloves. Security was concentrated on the exterior and perimeter. I had actually worked up a sweat playing around. "Nah, my man. You won't see me tomorrow. You get today only."

San Antonio freaked. Tried to back his wheelchair away, but had locked the wheels. Fool almost flipped. "What do you want?"

"Glad you remember me," I said, donning the accent I'd used in Vegas during our meeting. "The better question is what you want with me."

"Nothing. I don't want a thing. You've done enough," he said, shuddering as I came closer.

"You're trying to blame your predicament on me? I just gave you what you wanted."

"I . . . I didn't want *this*."

"I'll make it quick then. Who did you send looking for me?"

"No one. I'm not—I mean . . ."

"You told someone about me," I answered for him. "Bad business, Mr. Jackson."

"I had no choice."

"We always have choices. I just didn't think Andre Martin had it in him to be knee-capping folk to get info."

San Antonio laughed nervously. What I said amused him. "You're right. He doesn't. This here," he said, motioning to his legs, "this is from someone else that got riled up."

"Because of the photos?"

"Yeah," he said, glaring at me accusingly. "You brought down a ton of shit on me. I didn't pay for *this*, man. This is my career."

"Who?"

"I don't know. Never seen them before. Honestly. Some thugs. Rolled up on me leaving the store. Took me somewhere. Thought I was going to die. I'm no punk though. Didn't talk at first, but they threatened my wife. *After* they fucked me up."

"You still love her," I muttered. If someone threatened Collette, I don't know what I'd say or do. That woman had become my life, so I understood where San Antonio was coming from.

"Fuck yeah. And she loves me. I know that now," he said, his voice faltering just a bit. "Andre was a distraction because I wasn't doing what I needed to be doing."

"Andre hired those thugs?"

"I doubt it. He's been crushed since I sprung your surprise on him. His heart isn't in anything anymore. You delivered what I paid for, but now I don't know if it was worth it. Maybe I should have just talked to him," he said, shuddering as his eyes drifted off beyond me. He then returned to the present. "You've got somebody else riled up with those photos, and what they did to me is nothing compared to what they want to do to you."

"Do I look scared, Mr. Jackson?"

"From my vantage point, you should be."

I dropped the landscaper's blower I'd borrowed on his deck. "Be well, Mr. Jackson," I said, genuinely meaning it as I hopped down onto the lawn to leave.

"You too, sir."

"Sir, could you return your seatback to the upright position?" the flight attendant requested of me. We were on approach, descending into Dallas after our three-hour flight from Cleveland. Should've taken a few connecting flights and switched airlines, but I was weary. The hows and whys I was wrangling with in my head had nagged me since leaving San Antonio Jackson's home.

Before I left, I'd asked him a final question: Could he describe any of them that did the number on him?

He couldn't—except for one. The only one who didn't care if San Antonio could ID him. One who knew he wouldn't dare. One who wore a pendant that dangled in front of San Antonio's face while he threatened to do all sorts of things to the man's wife.

A pendant of a werewolf.

I returned back to my seat, knowing I'd been unable to relax the entire flight.

Chapter 29

Loup Garou.

Fuckin' Loup Garou.

Uncharacteristically, I lashed out, kicking the newspaper stand after deplaning.

"Hey! You wanna watch it!" the squatty worker yelled. Last thing I needed was an airport incident.

"Sorry. Just got some bad news," I replied as I hastily walked away.

I'd protected Penny Antnee in those photos, so there was no way he and his people could be all up in this. Unless Andre Martin ran to Penny and told him. Or maybe Penny heard about the photos and figured he'd clean up things on his own . . . just in case. But he wouldn't know to go after San Antonio unless Andre told him or San Antonio had bragged about it.

So which was it? Chicken or egg? Rock, paper, or scissors?

A mad one was I, both in anger and state of mind. Shit was deeper than I thought, and I couldn't leave the terminal without knowing more.

An Asian man in his twenties, hip and of vintage denim, sat cross-legged at his gate while scrolling through images on his laptop. The writing on his jacket was in Chinese, so I took a gamble that he was waiting to return to Taiwan.

"*Who ker yee chia nee ter xi shang xing dian nao ma?*"

He reacted as he would in his country, looking to see who was making the request to borrow his computer. Then he recognized my face as not that of a countryman.

"Did you say what I thought you said?" he asked in his best classroom English.

"I certainly hope so," I replied with a smile. "Otherwise I profusely apologize. May I borrow it? Please."

"Sure," he said with a shrug as he reached up and passed it to me.

Paying for Internet in the airport leaves a record, and I didn't want any government agency correlating movements and expenses of any names I operated under. I pulled up 4Shizzle's Web site on a hunch, thinking it, TMZ, or Media Takeout would be the places for gossip of the sort I suspected was in the wind.

When the front page of 4Shizzle displayed, I was greeted by a cherry bomb with a lit fuse—their idea of breaking and potentially explosive news. Being responsible for a few of their big stories, I was familiar with this format. I took a deep breath and clicked on the image, preparing myself for whatever story they were running.

I was greeted with:

BREAKING NEWS:

IS NFLER ANDRE MARTIN PLAYING WIDE RECEIVER TO WELL-KNOWN RAPPER?

YOU DECIDE.

Timing was everything in their business. I couldn't have arranged it any better myself. Beneath their banner was an unaltered photo, Penny Antnee's prominent tat visible and on full display. Couldn't mistake the camera angle either. It was one of my photos from the room in Vegas. The ones I hadn't shared with anyone.

"*Xie xie*," I said, handing the gentleman his laptop after deleting the website from his history file. I moved faster through the airport now, feeling equal parts rage and anxiety. My sloppiness had exposed me. I searched my phone for a number I had never used.

Dialing *67 first, I placed a call to the editor of 4Shizzle. She'd given it to me early on in our business relationship, but I valued the buffer of the Internet. That buffer be damned tonight; directness was needed to get these answers.

The mysterious editor picked up, rambling. "Not too many people have this number, so you can make me guess who this is, although I'd prefer not to."

"Pull the photo."

"You finally pick up the phone to call me and it's over a photo?" she teased, declining to play dumb. She knew it was me and that posting it would get this kind of reaction.

"Pull it."

"Why would I? It's not like I got it from you anyway. You sent me that doctored shit, remember?"

Without admitting I was the owner, I asked, "Who'd you get it from?"

"Can't say. Sources 'n all that stuff, love."

"Was it was a woman?" Sophia. Had to be, I thought, remembering the mistake I made by bringing her to my site.

"If that's not the big story you're after, then why publish it?"

"Because it's a step toward something," she offered. "A much bigger story. Something way

more interesting than Penny Antnee or who he's fuckin'."

"Indulge me then. What's the bigger story?"

She giggled. Not the harmless kind. "You," she replied.

I caught myself, almost walking in front of a passing taxicab on my way to the airport garage.

"Hello? You still there?"

"Yeah. I'm here."

"Remember when I told you I'd make you famous? Well, you're going to make me famous. You really should've taken me up on those offers to talk when you had the chance."

"You don't know me. You don't want to know me," I threatened, my voice dropping an octave.

"Are you sure I don't? What's the weather like in Dallas?"

I looked up at the billboard welcoming visitors to the Dallas-Fort Worth Metroplex. I'd landed in a web, not knowing who was doing the spinning. "Next time I go there, I'll let you know," I replied.

"Aww, c'mon." She laughed. "Like they say, the *truth* will set you free."

Chapter 30

"Is any of this your doing?" I asked, quickly shifting the Audi TT down Highway 183 en route back to my place.

"Hello to you as well, nephew," Jason scoffed. "What are you accusing me of this week?"

"I'm not accusing. I'm just asking," I said, easing off my accusatory tone. More flies with honey and all that.

"Will you persist with being vague, or will you spit it out? I have much on my plate at the moment and nothing to hide on my end." That meant he had nothing to do with it directly, but he still may have known something of my predicament.

"Anyone being nosey on your end?"

"About some photos?" Yeah. He knew all about it.

"About anything," I answered. "Heard anything? Know anything?"

"Why would I? It seems you might have had something extra as a result of our most recent arrangement and chose not to share. Didn't the purple dinosaur teach you, nephew? Caring means sharing."

"Look, you got what you paid for. Anything else was mine to do with as I saw fit."

Jason chuckled. "And I see where that's gotten you."

"So you do know something."

"Certain people are asking certain things."

"And?"

"And I'm not quite sure how to answer, dear boy. I'm making major moves in this industry which call for new alliances and new considerations."

"Alliances and considerations that could be detrimental to me?"

"Hey, you told me yourself that our relationship is over, that we are done. Count yourself fortunate that I discussed this much over the phone, son."

"Indulge me one more question," I requested.

"It's your last chip. Place your bet."

"The girl I was with in Vegas."

"The stunning beauty that still haunts my illicit dreams? What about her?"

"Did she have any kind of side deals with you?"

"Honestly, no. But seeing as how she's on your mind at a time like this, I sincerely wish she had."

"Fuck you," I said, not knowing whether to believe his answer.

"Be well, nephew. And don't call me again. With these new *friends* of yours, you're too hot to deal with. I take great joy in being the one to say that we're done."

After the finality of our conversation, I decided to turn to Collette, as she might have some valuable information on Sophia. Of course, any chance to see her made me happy. As observant as she was, I had to be careful to conceal what a predicament I found myself in and shield her from it at the same time.

From Oak Lawn, I took a right onto Lemmon Avenue, speeding past William B. Dean Park when I saw flashing lights ahead. I pulled over in front of Hook, Line & Sinker to observe without getting too close to the action.

The flashing lights were from police cars stationed outside a building down the street.

I felt bile creeping up in the back of my throat as I processed what I saw. Remembering what had been done to San Antonio Jackson, a wave of nausea overcame me.

The police were at Collette's place.

Chapter 31

I walked hurriedly down the sidewalk toward the two police cars next to the curb, keenly aware of every face, every stranger I passed. I was material, no longer that unknown figment to everyone. That meant I could be touched; could be harmed.

Or hurt through others.

I passed the open gate to Collette's stairwell, dialing her number first. After all, the police could be there for another resident. All she had to do was answer and I could calm down for now.

But she didn't answer.

I hung up, deciding to risk any threat that might await me. Spinning, I reversed direction and headed for her stairwell. Skipping two and three steps at a time, I quickly darted to the top. I tried to breathe deeply, to prepare myself for whatever awaited me. Turning the corner, I bumped into two officers as they left.

"Sorry," I said, not making eye contact. I over-heard them saying the other officer could handle this, whatever it was. That had me calmed, until I saw Collette's door ajar, its frame smashed. I rushed in and was greeted by still another officer. The tall, crisp brother almost drew his gun on me.

"Sir, do you live here?" he asked by the book. Kane was the officer's name.

"What happened?" I asked, surveying the strewn-about plants and dismantled book shelf. The rage that had subsided was roaring back. I stepped over a broken piece of ceramic.

"Collette!" I yelled.

"Sir, I'm going to have to ask you to step back," he urged. I ignored him, wondering where Collette was and if anything had happened to her on my account.

"Collette!" I called out again. Somebody had connected me to her and this place. Knew that much as sure as the sun rises in the east and sets in the west. Had to be Sophia, but would she expose her own flesh and blood to people like this?

"That's it. Put your hands up and step back!" he yelled, his gun now drawn and pointed at me.

"Where is she?" I asked, ignoring the peril. I raised my hands to show him I had no weapons and meant him no harm.

With his gun still drawn, he reached up with his free hand, preparing to radio in that he had a situation. Being a good officer, he was probably committing my features and description to memory. Made me regret not disguising them before I came here. I began debating whether to disable him or simply run for it. Collette's unknown status made me freeze instead.

"Officer, it's okay. He's my friend," Collette said as she emerged with her cane. She reached out to touch something, but it wasn't there, obviously moved or destroyed in whatever had taken place. I wanted to go to her and take her hand, but the officer's gun was still drawn. The only plus was that he'd released the button on his radio for the moment.

"What's your name?"

"Chris Davis," I replied innocently, hoping that he wouldn't ask for some ID. The only one I had in my suit belonged to a different name— one I'd used to travel to Cleveland and back. "May I help her?" I asked, motioning with my hand about her visual impairment and current predicament.

He hesitated, but holstered his weapon as I knew he would. Breathing a sigh of relief, I thanked him and went over to take Collette by her arm. Instead she hugged me tightly.

"I'm so glad you're here," she said, exhaling deeply as her pent-up emotions passed over me like a tsunami. "Where have you been?"

"I was out taking care of some business. Sorry I wasn't here for you."

"Do you know anything about what happened here?" the officer asked, a report form having replaced his sidearm in his hand.

"No," I replied, although he was waiting on human nature to make me volunteer further, even if I knew nothing. I'd faltered, but was back on my game. "Do you?" I asked back.

"Break-in, looks like." He sighed. "We don't usually get these kinds of calls around here. Somebody was looking for something or someone. Don't think they found what they were looking for."

"I was so afraid," Collette offered. "I screamed at the top of my lungs when I heard them."

"Hold up," I stated, cutting her off. "Do you know for certain it was more than one person?"

"Pretty sure," she replied, touching her ear. The officer and I both understood. "I was in my bedroom. I got to my door and locked myself in. They just kept breaking stuff. I have the police on speed dial, so I curled up behind my bed and waited. Chris, I . . . I thought—"

"Shhh. It's all right," I cooed. "You're okay now."

"When we got here, we found the place like this. My unit was nearby, so we may have chased them off before—" He caught himself, realizing he wasn't making things better. "I recommend that she get the door secured and stay someplace else. She shouldn't be alone, sir."

"She won't be," I assured him.

While Collette finished giving her story to the officer, I went to her bedroom to retrieve a few things. At her bedside was a framed photo, something that wasn't present during my previous times shared with her in here. It was of her and her husband, somewhere on a cruise during a different period of her life. Like some of her old books, a remnant from times of sight. She probably placed it in the drawer when I was around. Still had feelings for him, but why wouldn't she?

I felt regret, worrying about her paying the ultimate price for another miscalculation of mine. Right there, I vowed to a ghost of her past that I would be the guardian of her future. After we got maintenance to make some temporary repairs, I took her with me, careful that we weren't followed.

"Have you talked to Sophia lately?" I asked, driving in circles just to get to my apartment.

"You're always asking about her. Damn. If I didn't know any better, I'd swear the two of you had something going on."

"Highly unlikely," I responded. "You said so yourself that she had some questionable doings in her life. I'm just wondering if she had anything to do with this."

"Why would my cousin have anything to do with my break-in?"

"I don't know. Just a feeling."

"For someone you barely met, you sure have a low opinion of her."

I shook my head, frustrated with the quandry I found myself in. If she'd known what Sophia was capable of, she'd probably agree with me. Of course, knowing that would expose a different side of me to Collette also. A no-win situation.

"Don't mean to be hard on your blood, but—"

"I haven't heard from her. There," she spat out, cutting me off.

"And you're sure you don't know where she's at?" I pushed on. She had no idea how serious this was. Penny Antnee and his people were gunning for me, probably because of what Sophia had done. And from what they did to San Antonio Jackson, there was no limit to their ruthlessness.

Collette sighed. "Is your novel a crime drama? Because you sound like you're interrogating me right now."

"Sorry. I'll back off. I'm just wondering if somebody she knew is responsible."

"Your guess would be as good as mine, Chris."

But I didn't have to guess. "C'mon, let's get you to my place," I said as we made our final lap around Uptown.

Chapter 32

Opening the door to my place, I let Collette in first, sliding her bags off my fingers and onto the floor. She took a few steps, her cane tapping a clear path ahead before she stopped.

"You're not going to leave me alone here, are you?" she asked, turning her head back to where I stood.

"I just need to run downstairs for a moment. You're safe here," I said, not fully believing it. Somebody had connected the dots. It was only a matter of time before a direct line led here, in spite of my changing apartment units. I needed to get out of Dallas altogether and take Collette with me. Breaking cold, hard facts like that to her would be tough. Both the creation Chris and my real persona were liabilities at the moment, thanks to Sophia. If Penny and his boys had some kind of code, I could just disappear and they'd leave Collette out of it.

But they didn't. And they wouldn't leave her out of it. Not now. She was my kryptonite crack, capable of rendering me a mere mortal, but that which I couldn't live without.

I took Collette by the hand and led her to my sofa. I sat with her for a moment, brushing her hair aside. "I have a package downstairs waiting on me, but I want you to know that I'll be right back, I swear. I promised I'd protect you, and that's what I'm going to do."

"Who?"

"Huh?"

"Who'd you promise, Chris? Who'd you make that promise to?"

"Oh," I replied, fumbling for a second. "Myself. I just meant—"

"Do those people that broke into my place have to do with Sophia . . . or you?" she asked, cutting me off in mid-lie. She moved her body away from me in a way she never had before. The one person I cared for was being driven away with every deceptive utterance.

"I just know they're dangerous, Collette," I answered with a non-answer. "We need to talk about it . . . as soon as I come back up."

"Go on, Chris. Go get whatever is so important," she said, waving her hands in disgust. "Maybe it'll give you time to come up with some real answers."

I got up from the sofa, knowing better than to reach out to her at the moment. She was right though. Maybe I would have some answers when I returned. I grabbed a nearby backpack and left for the lobby, taking with me a computer that had probably been compromised at some point.

In the lobby, I sat in an empty chair near the front desk, retrieving my laptop from the bag while watching for anything unusual that might creep up. While the Windows symbol greeted me, I placed a call to California, the true reason I had for getting away from Collette.

"Agent Fuentes," the parole agent answered.

After greetings were exchanged with Dom Fuentes, I took him back down memory lane, to a past job I'd done for noble purposes, but one that would still cost him his job if anyone knew. When I was done reminding him, he agreed begrudgingly to cooperate with my simple, lone request.

"Whatchu got?" he asked.

"African American female, first name Sophia, probably born and raised around Inglewood. Driver's license says her last name is Williams and she lives in Santa Monica, but it's probably a fake. She's done some modeling before. No visible scars. Tiny heart tat around her waistline. Probably served time in the past five years, maybe had a male partner/accomplice in some kind of scheme," I rattled off.

"Do you have her accomplice's name or a last known address?"

"No," I embarrassingly admitted.

He sighed, perhaps sensing his job might be in jeopardy if successful with my request. "Do you at least have a visual for me?"

"That, I can accommodate." I provided Agent Fuentes with a description of Sophia, minus the lurid details I was privy to, and sent an e-mail to his personal account with Sophia's image from her night with Natalia. From a quick check, it seemed my files were only copied rather than stolen. Besides, if Sophia somehow had the ability to monitor my online activity, I wanted her to know I was coming for her first chance I got.

Dom acknowledged receipt of the photo. "Look, I'll see what I can do. No promises," he offered.

"Just hurry. I need to know if she's reporting in to you guys and where she's currently staying. She might've had a temporary address in Dallas earlier this year."

"Then we're through?"

"Yes," I said as something on the mounted flat panel TV above me caught my eye. "If I don't an-swer, just leave the info on the voice mail."

Bad-boy football player Andre Martin had crashed his car in the wee morning hours, going through a guard rail and down a ravine. Dead. Claimed there was alcohol on his breath. All the bad luck befalling the Oakland team was the chief topic these days, and the new rumors swirling about Andre's sexuality had been the cherry on top. Now this tragedy was being milked by the media wolves for all it was worth.

I knew Collette must've been on pins and needle, but I quickly jumped on the net. 4Shizzle was offering condolences to Andre Martin, all the while teasing a blockbuster story about a man behind the scenes of so much out there. Ballsy.

I sent a message to the editor via our standard means of communication:

> *Last chance to stop. It would be in your best interests. You have no idea how bad it could get.*

She didn't reply.
So be it.
I ended the fruitless connection, preparing to shut my laptop down and return to Collette when my alarms went off. I spied two people who stood out by the desk: one large, one small. The diminutive one made me more wary as he asked questions of the man at the desk.

Without it completely depowered, I slammed the lid on my laptop and stood up.

". . . went by his old apartment, but he's not there. We wanted to surprise Chris while we're in town. Do you know where he moved?" I caught coming from the small visitor as I walked by, headphone earbuds inserted and bobbing my head, but with no music playing. The man at the desk was new, and fortunately didn't know the tenant "Chris" by sight.

I closed my eyes behind the sunglasses I'd thrown on, glad I'd switched apartment units on a hunch, but desperately hoping the deskman wasn't an idiot.

"I'm not supposed to provide that kind of information, *but* since you're his boys," he volunteered, eager to be down and oh-so-helpful. I didn't wait to hear him give me up to those who would be my killers.

Probably the same ones that killed Andre Martin.

Chapter 33

Inside the elevator, I pushed the button for my floor, remaining icy calm to the uninformed passerby. Inside, my heart threatened to erupt from my chest as I waited for the doors to shut. The two men from the front desk joined me before it closed. Shit. I had terrible luck with elevators.

"What floor?" I asked, settling on the direct approach. I took on the affect of a Midwestern brother straight out of college who chose to party too hard. If I were lucky, they hadn't been sufficiently briefed on who they were searching for.

"Twelve," the stubble-faced one muttered. Looked to be Armenian. Would Penny pay for something of this caliber? I punched the button as instructed. They hadn't realized it was already pushed when they entered. They were certainly looking for me. I followed by pushing number fourteen as if it were my floor.

The small one spoke into his cell phone. "Yeah," is all he said, replying to someone giving orders. I kept pretending to listen to music, as if I were someone other than whom they sought. A target in plain sight posing as an obstacle, I shifted my weight and altered my stature, willing myself into another person entirely. What used to take days of rehearsal, I could now do in minutes if it called for it. I just prayed this time was academy worthy.

"Man, did y'all go to Republic last night?" I asked, referring to the loud, trendy bar that I could sometimes hear from my balcony. "They had the bitches. Man, I'm still tryin' to sober up."

They ignored me, focused instead on the escalating numbers as the elevator approached my floor. I could almost see the gears turning in their heads as they game-planned for whatever might go down. High quality suits they wore, again not jiving with Penny Antnee or what he'd associate with. You'd never guess they were on a mission with bad intentions by the way they coaxed my whereabouts downstairs. Well-paid and well-trained. I wondered if they were the same ones who busted up Collette's place, or whether they had teams combing through Uptown.

"Y'all not cops, huh?" I asked in an intentionally noisy whisper. I strained my voice to add to the illusion that I'd been yelling all night. "Y'all look like cops."

The short one looked at me this time, shaking his head in the negative. From behind my sunglasses I grinned, while watching the numbers close on twelve.

"Good!" I shrieked, becoming more obnoxious as we got closer to my floor. "Y'all want some X? 'Cause I got the good stuff in my bag right here, y'know? And I'm cheaper than those bastards on the third floor."

"No, thanks," the stubble-faced one replied with a slight laugh. His guard was down now. And they'd reached my floor. The doors began to open and my options were few.

I crouched down, taking my earbuds out and reaching into my backpack. "Jus' . . . jus' let me show you, man. I even do bulk discount if you wanna party. Avon ain't got shit on me."

"Go away," the small one said without looking at me, his mind entirely on business.

"Suit yourself," I said as I took a secure grip on my laptop. They were both threats, but I had to choose quickly. Throwing all my weight behind it, I swung my laptop into the larger one's prominent nose, driving him to the back of the elevator car. I threw my leg around, kicking the small, shifty one in his chest. He went spilling into the hallway as I swung my laptop over my head in an arcing motion to connect atop his partner's head again. The direct strike was a finishing blow for him, as he crumpled before he even had a chance to defend himself.

I didn't have time to celebrate, as the one in the hallway proved just how deadly they were. As quick as I suspected he was, he'd drawn his gun, just missing my head with his first silenced shot. I yelped as it sparked off the elevator wall, turning my laptop just in time to shield me from the next one.

And the next one came, striking me dead in my chest, if not for the miraculous piece of technology that was my connection to all.

Was.

I would come to regret that my laptop was destroyed, but praised the most basic purpose it served at this moment. I darted to the side of the elevator car to avoid giving him another clear shot. Any element of surprise I had was quickly fading. As good as I was at what I did, he was equally good at his craft.

Figuring I was their immediate target and not Collette, I played into that and rapidly pushed the button to close the elevator doors. He fired a wild shot, striking his unconscious partner—killing him on the spot, based on the entry point. I jumped to my feet, pressing myself against the wall as much as I could. As the doors were almost completely shut, I knew he couldn't chance my slipping away.

He could risk pressing the hallway button and hope it would stop my car, or he could do that which I hoped, the more immediate solution.

He inserted his gun, silencer first, unloading where I'd just stood. I risked all, diving toward the muzzle as it exploded, but higher than his calculated aim. As the final shot rang out, he extended his arm further in. The doors were parting as I caught his arm, wrenching it backward as I flew in the other direction. I threw all my weight into it, hearing the sick snap as it banged against the retreating door. He fell over, writhing, and dropped his empty gun to grip his dangling, wounded limb. That left nothing to shield him from the hardest knee I could place to his exposed brow. On contact, his head snapped up, his eyes rolling back as he went to sleep.

As the doors attempted to shut on him, I dragged his limp body fully inside to join the dead man. Before leaving them and allowing the elevator to continue on its ascent to the fourteenth floor, I smashed their cell phones. I was running down the hall before I remembered my shot-up laptop had been left behind; something that could be a costly error. Things had gone from bad to worse.

"Chris, what's wrong?" Collette asked as I entered my apartment in a hurry, slamming the door behind me.

"Baby, we have to go. Now," I answered, gasping for air and trying to steady myself as the adrenaline fled my body.

Chapter 34

I swerved over the line, avoiding a crossing armadillo that may or may not have been there. A hazy cloud enveloped my mind at the moment; a product of hours behind the wheel of a slow-moving truck. Collette was jarred from her fitful slumber by the sudden sway.

"Sorry about that," I offered, too guilty to look at her.

"Fuck you, Chris," she spat. "If you were sorry, you'd tell me where you're taking me. Or at least bring me back home."

"Can't do that, but I can tell you we're going somewhere safe."

"Like your place was supposed to be safe? I should just jump out," she countered. It woke me up. Made me focus as I questioned how serious she was about hurling herself from the vehicle.

"You might want to reconsider. We're doing seventy miles per hour," I said.

"Bullshit. From the way the engine's straining, you're having trouble keeping it over fifty."

I glanced at the speedometer, grimacing as it sputtered out around fifty-three. "You'd still hurt yourself. Look . . . can you cut me some slack?"

"My back is killing me in this awful seat, and I have to pee again. Don't you dare talk to me about slack."

We'd been on I-20 for longer than I'd care to admit, stopping only for gas and bathroom breaks at the smallest of gas stations, those less apt to have surveillance. Half that time was spent getting Collette to calm down and trust me somewhat. I constantly checked the rearview mirror of the oil field truck I'd "borrowed" back in Colorado City. It'd be at least a week before they noticed an abandoned Audi left in an old barn off the highway. When they found it, they would also find the bag of Collette's things I'd left by accident. I didn't dare break it to her that she wore the only set of clothes we had in the truck.

My current diet consisted of Red Bull and pepperoni sticks. Any time I wanted to nod off or let my guard down, I just had to think back to the unlucky one in that elevator back in Dallas. His death and my narrow escape left me with only enough time to snag some emergency cash. Low on options, I was going to the only safe place I'd known, taking a journey back in time.

"If you have to go, I'll pull over."

"If I have to go," she repeated, mimicking me robotically. "What's wrong with you? Ever since you yanked me out of your apartment scared shitless, it's like you're another person, Chris."

"It might be best if you don't call me that anymore," I solemnly warned.

I'd caught it on the small TV back at the Conoco in Abilene. Chris was being sought for questioning in the murder of a businessman and possible kidnapping of a blind woman in Dallas. But not everyone was so blind. That officer had seen me at her apartment, so they'd have a sketch connecting me to both events.

All this shit was being intentionally laid at my feet. They knew the authorities wouldn't find Chris. But they might find Collette, and in that, a way of tracking me down. Maybe once I had some breathing room, I could negotiate. Thing is, something kept nagging at the back of my head, telling me I was more lost than ever.

"Was it an accident?"

"Huh?" I asked with a stutter, replaying the errant bullets burrowing into my would-be assassin's body as I ping-ponged around the elevator. I hadn't shared it with her, hoping to postpone it until a time when I could rationalize everything.

"That we met," she answered, either voluntarily turning toward me for the first time or simply repositioning herself in the seat. Regardless, I looked at her. She was absolutely breathtaking, a soothing melody in the middle of a noisy, loud, screaming, terribly bad world.

"I'd like to think it was fate," I said, smiling for the first time since our journey began.

The road sign said forty miles to I-10 and one hundred twenty miles to El Paso.

It must've been an omen, for steam and smoke shot out from under the truck's hood. I shook my head in disbelief, powerless to do anything as we sputtered to a halt.

"Good luck with y'all's truck," the towering man in the Vietnam Veterans baseball cap said as he stopped at the red light just off I-25.

"Thank you much, sir," I replied with a polite nod of my head as I helped Collette down.

The fortuitous eighteen-wheeler had come along, delivering us to our final destination. Rather, delivering me and my sister, Nolene, who was recovering from Lasik surgery when our truck broke down on our way to our mom's. I advised Collette to wait for the truck to disappear back on I-25 before using her walking stick. She'd heard every word I'd uttered, reserving her comments until now.

She shook the collapsed white wand, allowing it to unfold in her hand. She tapped it once to the pavement for certainty. The multi-colored dress she'd worn since my apartment was terribly wrinkled. In spite of her attire, her elegance was in no way diminished. "It's so easy to you," she said.

"What?"

"Lying." She said it with utter contempt, the polar opposite of the admiration expressed by her cousin Sophia at my ability.

"I'm just trying to protect us. Somebody out there has bad intentions, so I'm in survival mode. Forgive me for not wanting anything to happen to you," I chided.

"You just don't stop," she sang. "If that was true, then why don't we just go to the police?"

"Maybe in your world. In mine, they can't be trusted. Not with something like this," I said, surveying the well-worn streets leading to our temporary home.

"It's you I'm about out of trust with."

"It won't make things better, but I'll explain it all. C'mon. Let's get off the street. I've got somewhere to freshen up and get some rest."

"Do you have my bag with you?"

I didn't reply, instead postponing the full wrath of a woman stranded in New Mexico without a change of clothes. Without delay, I led Collette a few blocks to an aging hotel on the edge of the small town.

Chapter 35

"We're not in Texas anymore, are we?"

"Neither are we in Kansas, Toto," I joked, trying to add some levity to a dire situation. Didn't work so well. Exposing so much to Collette made me nervous, something I wasn't accustomed to feeling.

"You're neither cute nor funny, Chris—or whatever you want me to call you. Asshole will do?"

"Okay, I deserve that. We're in New Mexico, if you must know," I replied as I opened the front door to an establishment for her and to a previous chapter for me. The hotel still had that tacky red interior that I remembered, albeit less cared for. My mom told me she found this place by accident, when she meant to stay on I-10 in the storm, but made a wrong turn in her undependable car. She wound up at the Asilo Rojo Inn, arriving in this very lobby with a world of problems and a bellyful of hell spawn that was me.

The elderly man at the counter smoked a cigarette, while a tiny woman vacuumed. He muttered something while folding over the pages of his newspaper. Thought he would've been dead by now, yet there he was.

"*¿Cómo estás, Daniel?*" I asked as I approached.

"What do you want? Do I know you?" he asked, not really expecting customers. I could tell the nicer spas and lodges closer to town had supplanted his establishment as options for other than the most desperate of travelers. For me, this suited my needs.

"My mother used to work here," I answered formally, showing no love for the man who probably saved our lives back then and on whom I was relying now to shelter me and Collette from the brewing storm.

"Oh? What was her name?"

"Leila," I answered. I knew he had no other African American women ever working here, so that was merely for his satisfaction. I watched the smile slowly sweep across his face, exposing rotting teeth.

"Yes, I remember," he hissed, his Spanish accent thickening as it once was. Before me, his white hair transformed back to the solid ebony mane he previously possessed. His teeth fixed themselves, and his gut reduced by an inch or two. I was suddenly three feet tall before the man who merely tolerated me, due to his fondness for the exotic chocolate that was my mother, and because I stayed out of his way.

"How is she?" he asked, abruptly running his hands through his scraggly mane while examining the lobby further in hopes that she might be with me.

"She's doing fine," I answered matter-of-factly. "Married to a nice man. They live in a mansion in the Bay Area these days. Told her I might see you. Traveling around the country and figured I'd stop by. Need a room for a few days."

"Oh. I think we have some rooms. Especially for Leila's son. Josefina!" he yelled at the woman vacuuming before quickly shifting his focus back to me. "One bed or two?"

"Two," Collette interjected as I opened my mouth. One didn't need sight to know our relationship was disintegrating the longer this went on.

"Very well," Daniel the inn owner said, cutting his eyes back to me as if to say I was less than a man for letting her mouth off. "I'll give you our best *two bed* room then. Josefina, get the keys."

Realizing how thin the walls were, I turned on the TV. Collette, sitting on the bed farthest from the door, massaged her aching feet. "Was that

stuff about your mom true? Did she work here?"
she asked.

"Yes."

"I can't believe you never talked about her.
Wow."

"That's because she's dead."

Collette gasped before regaining her composure. "Are you telling the truth now? Not to be
rude, but—"

"Yes, I'm telling the truth. She died a long time
ago."

"I'm so sorry."

I picked at a loose thread on the scraggly
comforter I sat upon. "Don't be. You didn't have
anything to do with it."

"Why are we here?"

"It was nearby. And totally safe. Some people
might know about other places, so I just got you
out of there and ran. It's not you. It's me they're
after. But I can't risk them hurting you."

"How long do you plan on keeping me here?
The place reeks of old cigarettes and sex."

"I know. It's just temporary. Long enough to
regroup and make sure you're safe in all this
mess."

"You keep saying that. How do you know
they'd hurt somebody?"

I bit my lip. "Because somebody's dead already. Back in Dallas. Would've been me if things worked out as they planned. I'm sure it's the same people that broke into your place."

"Oh my God. What are you involved in? What kind of person are you?"

I got off my bed and went over to calm her down. Wanted to make her understand that although a demon, I'd changed . . . because of her. I had to change.

"Don't touch me!" she yelled over the audio of the television set. I backed off, pacing the floor instead of returning to my bed, the isolated isle in the room.

"Things were going too good. Didn't want things to change between us or weigh you down with my past," I muttered.

"What did you do?"

"Information. Information of mine got out because of somebody." I didn't dare open up about me and Sophia to her. Not with the fault lines forming across the room, threatening to erupt in a magnitude six quake. "Certain people who didn't want this to get out are now looking for the source."

"You."

"Exactly."

"Before my head explodes, I have to ask you, *is Chris even your real name?*"

I took a deep breath. "No. It's Truth."

"Truth? That's your name?" she asked, half smiling at the irony.

"For real."

"As in 'truth or dare' or 'the truth will set you free'?"

"No," I finally answered honestly, replaying this same scenario with her scheming cousin Sophia when I'd lied. "As in 'Truth or Consequences,' the name of this town. That's my full name—Truth or Consequences. For real. My mother named me for the place where she had me." I chuckled. "She was strange like that."

"I could see why you'd want to be called Chris," she stated dead-face.

"The town used to be called Hot Springs. My name could've been worse. Or I could've been born in Roswell." I hoped for some softening of her mood, but Collette remained steeled.

"How come you never told me any of this?" she asked, as if more disappointed parent than angry lover.

"Because you never would've let me into your life. And I was ashamed. I never planned for any of this to—I . . . I'm sorry."

"How did you come about this information that is causing all these problems?"

"On one of my research trips. It wasn't what I was looking for at the time, but I kind of stumbled across it."

"Research. So you *are* a writer? Is that part true at least?"

"Yes, I'm a storyteller," I said, fudging in a desperate attempt to keep any portion of our relationship intact. "But not a very good one."

"Don't you dare feel sorry for yourself," she spat. "After someone lost their life because of you?"

"Actually, the person that lost his life tried to kill me," I replied, keeping the obviously related departure of Andre Martin to myself. That was the most needless death in all this. And I don't think my life would've spared his. They wanted anybody that could verify that video gone, and that included one of the participants. Maybe keeping Collette in the dark about the particulars could keep her off that list.

"Shut up! Just shut up! I don't know how you can be so calm and matter-of-fact in the middle of all this. People want you dead and could've killed me. This is hard to digest, Truth. Were you ever going to tell me your real name?"

"We agreed to only share so much. Remember? Did I ever push you to talk about your—"

"My blindness?" she asked, cutting me off. "I knew it was a problem. It would be for any man."

"No," I replied. "I was going to say your husband. I don't care if you're blind or have three eyes. I love you, Collette."

She gasped.

"I saw your picture with him back at your place, when I got your things. I know I could never replace what you had. I just need to know if you love me now. Especially now."

"I can't answer that at this moment. Honestly. These past twenty-four hours have been crazy. This is a lot to drop on me. I . . . I need a good night's sleep. Then maybe we can talk."

"Okay. I can respect that. I have no choice. And I'll do whatever I can to get your life back to normal."

"I haven't known normal in years, but I appreciate that. Do you have my clothes handy? I'd like to wash up and get some sleep."

"Um . . . about your clothes."

Chapter 36

The two of us slept with only a meal of convenience store leftovers last night, too exhausted to forage after our impromptu trip. To make up for it, I got up at the crack of dawn and visited Daniel, convincing him to let me borrow his truck for errands.

I traveled first to the new Wal-Mart on the north side of T or C that he'd recommended. Definitely more conveniences than I remembered as a small child. As discreet as I could be in a town of just over six thousand, I slipped in to pick up some clothes and toiletries. Not knowing whether my accounts were being monitored, I stuck to the basics with my cash, delaying the purchase of another laptop for now.

Along my return route, I stopped at the Cuchillo Café on Broadway for a batch of breakfast tacos, hoping I hadn't kept Collette hungry for too long. Mindful of my speed, I made my way back to the motel.

Daniel was watering the barren planter box outside the office when I returned his keys.

"Thanks," I said, wanting to keep conversation to a minimum.

"How do you plan on leaving T or C without a car?" he asked.

"We have one. It just broke down. Should be fixed in a couple of days."

"That's how a lot of people come to be residents of this place, amigo," he joked. "Cars break down and they decide to stay. Good life here. Quiet. Thought your madre might stay."

I looked back at him, remembering doors being slammed on me as he and my mother "talked" in one of the rooms she was cleaning. Happened often. And almost every time, Mary would take care of me, dispelling any bad notions I had, shielding a young mind from some things a person did just to get by in the world. Years past, I wanted to pay Mary a visit, to thank her for what she did for me, but I learned she'd already passed away.

"I'm glad she didn't stay," I commented simply to spite him, conflicted in that my mother might still be alive . . . and I might have turned out different, if the town that named me had held its grip on her. But Leila Marie had dreams to chase. Better to run to her dreams then live with her nightmares, I guess.

Outside our room, I put down my grocery bags and such, scanning the parking lot for anything out of the ordinary before turning the key. I grinned, remembering pretending as a child that each motel room was a portal to another place and that keys such as the one in my hand were magical.

"Collette?" I called out upon entering our portal to a place of temporary safety. The curtains were still closed, and it took a second for my eyes to adjust. With the light of day beaming in, I grimaced at the old wood paneling that adorned the walls, and the dirty air vents overhead. Collette's dress was still on the floor beside her bed. I heard the rushing water coming from the bathroom, and set our breakfast on the wobbly table before bringing in the other bags. The TV was on the local news, just going to a commercial that teased an upcoming episode of *Access Hollywood*.

"I'm back and I brought food. Real food," I shouted over the din of the shower, continuing to give Collette her space. Most of the night, when I wasn't unconscious myself, I watched her sleep restlessly from my bed. I would've held her, tried to calm her, if sure it wouldn't have riled her up more. Once she was safe, I would be coming for those responsible.

In the meantime, I set out making Collette's surroundings more bearable, fishing items from the Wal-Mart bags. I was nearly finished when the shower ended.

"Truth?"

"Yeah, I'm here." I waited during the long pause that followed. I could hear her fumbling, but knew her terms from the beginning: *I'm blind, not helpless. A strong woman, not some porcelain object. When I need your help, I'll ask. If I'm about to break, I'll let you know.*

"Um . . . I don't know this place too well."

I peered into the cracked bathroom door. Collette stood in the old shower, her damp body in need of the towel that had slipped off the rack. Unaccustomed to the unfamiliar, she let out a deep sigh, causing her full breasts to rise and fall, while the leaky faucet drip, drip, dripped. She sniffled, trying to fight back tears, but flow they did. She quickly wiped them away, taking another deep breath.

"Need a hand?" I asked, making myself known.

"Yes. How long have you been standing there?"

"Long enough."

"Knew it. I smell salsa." She chuckled, pretending her emotional state was a trivial issue.

"Goes with the breakfast tacos I picked up. But if it's irritating your sensitive nose, I can throw it out," I teased.

"Don't you dare!" she scolded, color returning to her face. "As hungry as I am, you won't have to worry about whoever's chasing you."

"You're ready to eat, I take it."

"Duh. Can you hand me a fresh towel? My other one fell on the floor and I'm afraid of what might be down there."

"Smart girl," I said, grabbing another towel. I extended it in front of her to allow her to step into me. "Right in front of you. Now, watch your step out the tub."

Collette followed my advice, entering the towel, but continued until we wound up in an embrace. She relinquished her hold on the towel, instead placing her hands to my face. She knew it would fall if I chose, but I held it tight around her body. She read my face again, as haggard as it was, but this time with intimate knowledge she hadn't known before. I closed my eyes, shuddering at the notion of being laid bare before her touch, as delicate fingers processed and interpreted my features. Sensing my uneasiness, she pulled my face closer, drawing out the poison of my tortured soul with a succulent, forceful kiss.

"Thank you," she said.

"For what?"

"For protecting me."

"Thank you for not giving up on me," I responded, choking up. Then something almost foreign to me occurred.

"You're crying," Collette whispered, seeming fascinated.

"No, I'm not," I quickly said. "It's just sweat."

She touched the damp mark on my cheek, tracking it back to my eye. Its mirror image was on the other side of my face. She licked at it. "Don't be afraid to feel. I'm not going anywhere," she whispered in my ear, making my knees weak. She pulled the towel separating us from my hand. Let it fall on the questionable floor as she pressed harder against me. "Feel me, Truth," she voiced, ancient, primal . . . siren-like in her command. I couldn't help but to rise.

I reached down, touching her inner thigh with the back of my hand. My knuckles brushed back and forth, grazing her smooth skin ever so briefly. In response to my secret code, her legs parted ever so much, allowing me entry to her treasure. I used my index finger, probing first, rather than rushing in and raiding. I moved back and forth across the fold of her lips, stopping at her clit, which I gently coaxed. With each journey of my finger, Collette came, dampness descending. Her clit now plump like a Ball Park Frank, I slid my fingers inside her, eliciting the sweetest moan as her simmer rose to a boil. She wrapped her arms tightly around my neck.

When I found her spot, I pressed. Collette gasped, her bottom lip trembling, prodding me to kiss her. We meshed, in sync to the tango our tongues performed. Close. Hot. Intimate.

One.

I removed my fingers from inside her, placing them in her mouth. Together, we tasted of her nectar—she as she sucked from my digits, and me as I continued my plunder of her lust-covered lips.

"I . . . I can't stand it any longer," Collette said, gulping for air. The tiny bathroom was depleted of oxygen, consumed by the fire of attraction made white hot by our bond this day.

Taking her by the hand, I led her out of the bathroom. Her bed was transformed from this morning when she left it. It now had fresh sheets and a comforter I'd purchased from the store. Hastily lit candles permeated the air with soft, soothing smells I knew would ease her state of mind. Just my attempt at making this minute corner of the world better, rather than rending it asunder, as was my core instinct. I stood silent, letting Collette process what had occurred. She felt the comforter first, confused initially, before letting a smile crease her beautiful mouth. She'd already smelled the change in atmospherics, and put her hand over her mouth in shock.

"Truth, you didn't have to do this. This is so sweet of you," she gushed.

"I know we're in a dump, and this is just lipstick on a pig, but—"

"Shut up," she said. With one hand, she grasped the comforter and sheets I'd affixed and pulled them back. With the other, she took me by the arm and pulled me onto her private isle, where she fixed herself atop me. She was sharing. I was no longer isolated. "No apologies. No excuses. Not now," she chanted as my dick swelled between her legs.

I undid my belt, hastily sliding my pants and underwear down my legs. Collette leaned over me, sucking and kissing across my exposed abs and chest as she inched my shirt up. I gripped those hips, refusing to lose the intense sensation we were generating from contact. So hot and moist, she was. So determined, I was, to fill her void with all I had and then some.

When my shirt was over my head, Collette feasted on my neck, determined to leave the mark of young love, of passion, of hot nights in secret places, of steamy windows in backseats—things I may have had if I'd attended school, but was left only to read of. Until now, only the people I was portraying, the false shells I wore, had experienced intimacy of this level: beyond the mere physical.

I lifted Collette slightly to allow me to enter her, but paused.

"What? What is it?" she asked, her hips moving about as she waited to receive me.

"Want me to get a condom?" I asked, hesitating. I'd been tested and was clean, but people can be infected with things other than diseases, things such as a dark soul of which others should be spared.

"No, no," she said. "Put it in."

I entered, feeling the tremors ripple through her body and around my dick as she yielded. She was so wet and inviting that I had to focus to keep from losing myself. I took my thumb, nuzzling her clit as she learned my rhythm and matched it. Felt her tighten and release with each sensual bob of her body atop me.

"Oh, shit. Damn," I muttered, blinking rapidly as she took control. In spite of its new adornments, the bed was still long in the tooth. It protested, creaking and sproinging loudly as we tested its tolerance. When it wobbled some, I grasped its sides and held on.

"Mm-hmm," she replied, acknowledging the understood praise I'd given her. "Right there.

Right there. *Shit*! Right there," she chanted, licking her lips then smiling wickedly. Sweat drizzled down her sexy body and onto my hands as I grabbed her breasts. The harder I squeezed, the harder she came. Before she knew it, the orgasms removed all reason and control from her body, crashing her ceaselessly onto my dick over and over.

"I . . . I . . ." I honestly don't fucking know what I was trying to say.

"Truth, I . . . I . . . want to feel you come. Come . . . for . . . me," she panted in between the breathless incantations I'd stopped trying to understand.

I sat up, keeping Collette in my lap, then rolled her on her back. "Oh!" she gasped, taken aback as I placed her legs over my shoulders, bending her in half.

"You like?" I asked as I began bumping and grinding, pushing up deeper in her pussy each time.

"Yes," she gasped as I felt her ass cheeks quake beneath me.

"You want?"

"Uh . . . huh."

I plunged my tongue down her throat, kissing her passionately. With her feet pointed to the water-stained ceiling above, I pumped harder and harder, my balls slapping against her ass, damp from her ever-flowing honey. We continued kissing, afraid of getting off the rocket we rode to untold pleasure. But I knew eventually the rocket would explode, sending its cargo spewing into her intoxicating goodness.

"Oh, baby! Oh, baby! Yes, baby!" she cackled, relinquishing all control, giving up as she gave it up. From deep in my groin I knew it was coming. Torn between easing off or relinquishing control myself, I gave in to the latter.

"I! I! I . . ." My eyes rolled back in my head, giving the old bed a final loud creak as I exploded inside Collette. I let her legs down off my shoulders before collapsing beside her, totally spent and incoherent.

Unable to speak, we just lay there, drifting in and out of lucidity. Two rag dolls tossed haphazardly across the bed. Once able to move, we'd really need the now less-than-hot breakfast tacos on the table. Collette found enough energy to nudge closer, where she burrowed into my chest. I draped an arm around her, content to remain in the moment.

Not as much time had passed as I thought. *Access Hollywood* was still on television, the inflections in Shaun Robinson's voice keeping me from full-on REM. I was intent on ignoring

her, rather than getting up and looking for the
remote, when I picked up on the subject of their
feature story.

    Penny Antnee.

    I was awake.

Chapter 37

"And as we promised, here is our exclusive one-on-one interview with Penny Antnee, where he talks about his mega successful music career, his new multi-million dollar endorsement deal, as well as the rumors swirling around about him! We caught up with the rap superstar at the exclusive Sanctuary Camelback Mountain Resort in Scottsdale, where he was enjoying some downtime alongside his upcoming film co-star and newest rumored romance, Ana Andrews."

Here I was holed up like a fucking fugitive, being stalked like some dog, while he was chilling poolside in Arizona with a hot Hollywood starlet. A short flight and I could be there, putting a bullet in his head, straight-up New Orleans style, or having someone else to do it with a call or two. But I wasn't a killer. Killer of souls and destroyer of spirits, maybe, but not a genuine cold-blooded, straight to the grave killer. Perhaps I was more vicious in my methods, but that was neither here nor there. They threatened Collette, making me contemplate something outside my usual boundaries. But I didn't know if this would end with Penny. I needed certainty when it came to Collette before committing down that path.

Collette moved, stirred from her exhausted slumber, cuddling tighter before drifting away again. I went back to observing Penny, admiring the profound strides this simple gangster with simple rhymes had made in what was a finger snap in the life of an artist. I watched Ana Andrews, the allegedly insatiable yet brilliant actress who never quite broke through to critical acclaim, but who saw opportunity in the young buck seated beside her, and probably hoped it would reignite her career. Penny was no better, having ditched his "beard" Natalia for a full-length genuine cougar fur in Ana. With Ana Andrews, no one would dare to question his sexuality card. Maybe Penny was one of those in-the-closet homophobic brothers, deluding himself into thinking that what I caught him doing on video was an aberration, brought on by too much drugs or booze or both. Or maybe, since he was the giver rather than receiver, that he wasn't gay.

He was finally being asked about the Internet rumors surrounding him and the recently deceased Andre Martin. I used the remote, turning up the volume.

"Think I may have met Andre Martin once," he answered Maria Menounos in as angelic a manner as he could muster. Ana stayed there at his side, her arm foolishly wrapped in his, oblivious to the depths he'd go to protect his true face from the public. "Don't know where all these crazy rumors get started, but I hope they didn't contribute to the man's accident. It's sad. Some out there get joy in tearing people apart for no reason. It's like they're monsters. I mean, how'd they like it if the shoe was on the other foot? If someone was out there prying into their lives and making stuff up on them, bet they wouldn't like that at all."

"I'm not gay, but I'm not gonna even dwell on negativity. I gots no problems with the gay community. I'm just trying to move forward and put the haters behind me. Trying to get some of this paper, y'know? I got mouths to feed, and people really hungry. And I feel sorry for you if you tryin' to stop me."

He'd convinced me. Not by his wasted false words for the masses, but by the glimmer in his eye at the end. The way he looked into the camera. He was talking to me. Calling me out. The business with Andre Martin could sidetrack not only his short term hip-hop cred, but derail his long term goals in Hollywood and beyond if he lost believability. In spite of this deeper level of sophistication I hadn't credited him with, there was more. Beyond crazed, sycophantic head-busters like Loup Garou, the Haitian Werewolf and the rest of his posse, there was something eerily familiar with the tactics being used in pursuit of me.

After the commercial break, *Access Hollywood* continued their special coverage dedicated to Penny Antnee. "We all know Penny Antnee is known for his famously chiseled arms, but what you might be surprised to know is that he now has legs to match," Shaun Robinson teased. "Or should I say *LEG* as in the Loretta Entertainment Group, founded by ageless forward-thinking fashion designer and European mogul Antonini Loretta. That's right; Penny Antnee has signed a multi-million dollar recording and production deal with LEG. This is one of the first signings under LEG's new media division, NME, a division headed by none other than an often controversial figure in his own right, Jason North."

"Fuck me," I muttered as North's image appeared in a box over the entertainment reporter's shoulder.

"In a move that stunned many industry insiders, Jason North has assumed position as CEO of North Media Experience, or NME if you can't get enough of the acronyms. While assuming his new duties, Jason is also bringing his own label, On-Phire Records, onboard as part of what is sure to be a power player in the years to come.

"Again, *Access Hollywood* was on hand for an exclusive with Jason following this bombshell announcement. Our very own Billy Bush sat down with Jason at his new Manhattan offices to chat about his coup in signing Penny Antnee right out the gate."

I watched my uncle preen like a peacock, stroking his goatee as a new media darling in spite of the lives he'd ruined, many by my hand. Whatever he was about to say was certain to be sheer bullshit.

"As someone who's familiar with the streets out there and knows what these young men have to go through, I'm blessed to be at this point in my career, where I can try to lift up entire communities from this new platform," Jason crowed. "And with talented young men like Penny Antnee, there are limitless possibilities ahead. We just have to be sure not to let crazy rumors and innuendo detract from what we are trying to do."

And the missing pieces to the puzzle were suddenly found.

Now I understood how Penny Antnee's people were able to track me down in Dallas.

Opportunity.

"I'm starving," Collette said, glowing with a post-coital yawn and stretch. "Tacos are probably cold now, huh?"

I hit the power button on the remote. The screen faded to black as it went off, but I still saw Jason's smiling image.

"Don't worry. I'll warm them for you," I replied, holding at bay the white-hot fury building within me.

Chapter 38

"You're not eating?" Collette asked. She wore the new clothes I'd bought for her.

"No. Stomach's upset," I replied.

"Too many Chick-O-Sticks?" she followed up, pausing from gorging on her second warmed breakfast taco.

"I guess."

"Okay. What'd I miss?"

"What do you mean, baby?" I asked with a light chuckle to dispel her notions.

"Usually when I give a man some, he's less dour than you are. Something happened while I slept." Recent events had taken their toll on me. Left me careless, my poker face inadequate.

"Yeah," I acknowledged. "I had time to think about this mess."

"Whatever's meant to be, will be. An ulcer will do neither of us any good."

"True. But you certainly sound less stressed than before."

"What can I say? You gave me some. It made me less dour," she joked as she resumed her feast. I slid the salsa closer for her to dip. She smiled, sensing my observance. The woman had been pushed beyond the limits of most and still could hazard a smile. Amazing. She inspired even someone as irredeemable as me.

The magic boob tube moved beyond things of importance to Oprah sharing Dr. Oz and his magic colon diagram with us, but my mind was fixed on its previous gift. I now understood the game being played. My time around On-Phire gave me insight into Jason's sundry methods and motivations. He'd pitched his ability to sign Penny Antnee to LEG as leverage for them choosing him as CEO. Then he turned around, pitching his ability to solve Penny's problem—me—in exchange for signing with his new division. Jason, being the ultimate opportunist, probably recognized my handiwork from the swiped Vegas photos and gave me up, pointing Penny's people in my general direction to seal the deal.

And Penny had gone all out, unleashing the hounds.

Without realizing it, I'd been clenching and unclenching my fist, knuckles rapping repeatedly on the table. She had to have heard it, felt the vibrations through the table, yet said nothing.

"Hey, I gotta run down to the office for a sec. See if there are any messages," I offered up vaguely, finding myself needing some fresh air.

"Okay. But give me a kiss first." When I leaned across the table, Collette offered, "Just be careful. Okay?"

"I will."

I was dialing Jason's private number within mere steps outside the door. So frustrated was I that I dialed incorrectly, getting an error message the first time. I kept up my pace, ranging past the other units in quick succession. Instead of the office, I headed toward the pool on the opposite end of the building. A place I used to play. I dialed again as I approached the OUT OF ORDER—NO SWIMMING sign. This time, I dialed correctly, but it simply rang.

"Shit!" I cursed as I hung up and tried again. As it rang, I ignored the faded warning tape and walked to the edge of the drained pool. Someone answered as I stared down at the gunk and whatnot accumulated on the bottom through the years. Could've sworn I saw a rattlesnake slithering on about its business.

"Hello?" the soft female voice answered. Someone I'd never heard or spoken to before.

"Who's this?" I asked.

"You called," she challenged. "You should know who you're trying to reach."

"Put him on the phone now," I snapped. There was a pause, a moment where I waited for her to either hang up or comply with my demand. She did neither.

"Whoever it is that you're trying to reach, they are no longer taking calls on this number."

"Tell him I know. I figured it out. His deal. His part in this mess. Tell him he can stop them if he wants. Tell him that it would be in the best interests of all that he do so and quickly."

"This person to whom you might be referring wants to remind you of your choice to end the relationship. So you will simply have to live with your choice."

Live. She spoke of life, while wishing death. Mine.

"Is that it?"

"Yes. This number is no longer any good . . . for you or for him. Have a nice day."

Jason had cast aside the red flowing inside both of us in favor of the green that flows more readily on the avenues of power. Threats to the mysterious woman would do no good. "Fuck you," I spat right before she terminated the call. I had to deal directly with Penny Antnee, whether or not he was willing to listen. But before I came calling, I had to make sure Collette was out of the line of fire.

I imagined the pool as it was decades earlier, filled with water, pleasant, safe, complete. With a brief smile of remembrance and a sense of longing, I pivoted then headed back to the room. Perhaps T or C was a place to shield Collette, as it did for me as a small child, but getting her to agree to this might be next to impossible.

By the time I arrived back at our door, I'd gone through some scenarios concerning Collette. I was about to put my key in the lock when I realized the door was already open. Maybe I hadn't closed it properly on my way out and the wind had forced it open.

Collette was gone from the table, a breakfast taco left half eaten. Nothing seemed out of place from moments ago.

"Collette?" I called out, figuring she might be in the bathroom. The silence set me on edge again. With a quick check of the room, I went rushing out the door. The parking lot offered no clues as to her whereabouts, frustrating me more. With no other possibilities, I moved toward the office.

When I ran up to the front window of the motel, my fears subsided. Collette was inside, talking to Daniel at the desk. I swear I hadn't left her alone that long, and didn't know she could move that fast in an unfamiliar environment. Always something new to love about her. Daniel seemed more animated than usual. Could've been the mere presence of a pretty lady had his Latin blood pumping. If I could read lips, I would've just stood there and observed them a while longer. Knowing she was free from harm, I composed myself before joining them inside.

The bell jingled, signaling my entrance. They turned in my direction, abruptly ending whatever they were saying. The way Daniel's eyes darted from me to Collette and back again, I worried that maybe he'd pulled information out of her.

"No need to stop on my account," I offered, watching to see where things went from there.

"It's okay," Collette said. "Daniel was just telling me more about Truth or Consequences."

"*Sí*," Daniel added with a smile. "I was telling your lady friend about some of the places she might like to see . . . uh . . . experience." His head dropped in shame at the simple mistake. "I'm sorry, ma'am."

"It's okay," she said, accustomed to such stumbles. "Truth, Daniel recommended Elephant Butte Lake. Maybe we could go there."

"You remember Elephant Butte, huh?" Daniel asked of me.

"Never got to see it," I answered. "You kept my mother pretty busy, so she never really took me anywhere."

"Oh. Well, maybe I can make it up to you . . . for your madre. Take my truck whenever you'd like. I really think the beautiful lady would enjoy it this time of year."

"Thank you, Daniel. We might have to take you up on that."

I excused us, not fully sure I could trust him, and hastily led her back to our room. No woman likes being rushed. The "pissed-offedness" was evident in her face and her short, choppy breaths as she tapped her stick.

"Why were you in there?" I asked.

"You said you were going to the office, so I went there to find you. And I wanted to get some air anyway. Is there a problem with that?"

"No. Sorry. I took a walk. Guess I lost track of time."

"Apology accepted. But you have to make it up to me."

"How?"

She rested her head in my lap as we sat in the back of Daniel's old truck. It was comfortably warm at the lake named for the eroded volcano resembling an elephant that jutted up from its center. The cool random gusts coming off the reservoir fed by the Rio Grande kept us from sweating. Being her eyes, I'd carefully described everything I saw from left to right, from the cheery boaters to the majestic San Andres Mountains off to the east. In describing them, I learned to appreciate the beauty of the butterflies, the simple elegance of the birds soaring overhead, the fascinating land features created by centuries of change. Of course, I knew the subject would eventually get back to me.

"Tell me about your story. The one you've been writing," she said as I stroked her hair. There was still that big, shiny lie between us.

"It was on my laptop. All lost. When I get another, I'll get to work recreating it."

"Will your publisher give you an extension?"

"I suppose. It's not my highest priority right now."

"What is?"

"You. Staying alive."

"In that order?"

"Yep. You come first. Because I can't live without you," I volunteered in a moment that felt as if the world held its breath, listening.

"Tell me more about yourself, Truth. Any brothers or sisters?"

"No, not that I'm aware of." I chuckled. "Only child as far I'm concerned."

"Did you know your dad?"

"No," I answered as I stopped stroking her hair, the image of a man popping to the forefront in my head. "Did you?"

"Yes. He and my mother were together until my freshman year at TCU. That's when they let me in on the secret that they didn't particularly care for one another."

"Wow."

"That's what I said . . . and then some. Affected my grades for two whole semesters. I almost dropped out because of it."

"Where are they these days?" I asked, already knowing the answer, but playing the role. "Maybe you could stay with them until this—"

"Dead. They had me when they were older. Passed away within five months of getting divorced from one another."

"That's kind of eerie."

"Yeah. I had no one until I met my husband. My father was a serial cheater. I think Myron was too. Of course, he never admitted it. Sometimes I wonder if that had something to do with what happened to him."

"I'm sorry to hear that," I offered, reliving my first encounter with her husband's mistress.

Before everything ended in thunder and fury for Collette. My last encounter with my client had consisted of her clearing out her account and begging me to forget she'd even hired me. I didn't accept the extra money. "Do you miss him?"

"In spite of my suspicions? Yes."

"I understand. Sometimes just a sliver of love can sustain one's heart," I waxed as I resumed stroking her hair. Perhaps there was a writer in me.

"Truth?"

"Hmm?"

"Did you sleep with my cousin Sophia?"

I closed my eyes and answered, feeling the cool gust off the lake turn into a frigid arctic blast.

Chapter 39

There was a knock at the door. After a day at Elephant Butte then dinner in town, we had retired to our room.

"You wanna get that?" I groaned.

"No. You?" Collette mumbled from the other bed.

The knock came again. "Probably got the wrong room. They'll go away."

"Maybe it's Daniel."

"Why? I gave him his keys back."

"Maybe you left something in his truck."

I gave up stalling and shuffled to the door, tensing on the off chance someone had found us. I wasn't naïve enough to think Jason might not know how I got my name, or that I might fall back here in desperation. And that he wouldn't share this information with Penny Antnee.

"Who is it?" I yelled before placing my eye to the peephole or revealing my shadow under the door. No need risking a shotgun barrage. If no one answered, it was either a drunk or we were in trouble.

"It's Daniel," our friend the innkeeper called out. "Sorry to disturb you."

"Told you," Collette mocked as she found the strength to sit up.

Only then did I check the peephole to see a waving Daniel. I cracked the door, leaving the latch in place.

"Everything okay, man?" I asked. As I spoke to him, I was looking beyond to the walkway for any additional shadows.

"*Sí, sí*. No problems," he replied, smiling generously. "I wanted to know if you could help me with something tomorrow."

"Shoot," I commented inappropriately.

I heaved another of the heavy rocks over my shoulder. It landed near Daniel, where he placed it in the wheelbarrow. If a rattlesnake showed, I had a rusty shovel at the ready. "Go on, Truth. Help the man out," Collette had egged, putting me in this spot.

"Why now?" I asked, grimacing at the desert sun beaming in my eyes. Daniel was a hazy shadow above me, obscured by light as he watched from ground level.

"Just because. Guests don't stay long these days. They all go to the nicer hotels and spas closer to town. Except for a few truckers, most only want to rent by the hour. It is nice having a couple like you two around here," my elderly foreman admitted. "It made me think. Made me remember how this place used to look. Maybe fixing the pool will be a start in that direction. Get some kids and families coming. Maybe I too can be a success like your madre, Leila."

The reverence with which he spoke of my mother gave me pause. Made me reconsider his interest as being more than carnal back in the day. Made me regret telling him she was still alive. No matter though. Her tragedy wasn't his. In trying to hurt him, perhaps I'd spared him even more. I waded barefoot into the gunk on the deep end of the pool once more, shovel in hand and wiping the sweat away with a forearm.

"I hope getting this pool open brings you better times, Daniel. I mean that," I said, happy to be contributing to something positive.

"And thank you for doing this. I'm a proud man. It's hard to admit I can't do what I used to."

Continuing the task of cleaning out the pool, I pushed that cynical voice aside, whispering that Daniel was probably a rich tightwad who was getting free labor in exchange for the use of his truck. As I looked up and smiled at him, he threw a bottle of Gatorade to me, which I caught and drank from before throwing it back. He placed the bottle next to my cell phone, which I didn't dare leave with Collette. Even set to vibrate, she probably would hear it.

After several more hours, I was exhausted. Daniel helped me pull myself out of the pit that might someday provide happiness and fun once again.

"You are a hard worker," he commented. "Wish there were more like you."

"I'm not done," I said with grin, wishing that I were. "I gotta take a piss."

I hadn't drunk enough to need to pee, instead simply missing Collette and wanting a break from the heat. Just a quick check-in and I'd be back to finish what I started. I left my phone and my shoes at the pool, sparing them the dirt and sweat covering me from head to toe. Although I ached in areas I didn't know existed, I found my burdens and stress lessened in others. I'd sleep good tonight, comfortably in Collette's welcome company; then tomorrow I would plot and plan anew, back on my "A" game, and woe be to those who stood in my way.

Those uplifting thoughts put a smile on my face, ushering forth a whistle as I strolled down the walkway toward our motel room.

But I stopped whistling. The smile disappeared next.

A massive black truck had pulled up hurriedly outside our room, occupying two parking spots on the usually empty lot. Its engine still ran, and from the cracked passenger window, the dark outline of a muscled dog was unmistakable as it looked in my direction. I froze dead in my tracks. Weariness didn't dull the warning horns blaring in my head.

Those horns would be loud enough to rupture eardrums when I saw the two men approaching our hotel room door. They hadn't noticed me yet, the dirty barefoot urchin that I was at the moment, certainly not what they would be looking for. But Collette was in there. There was at least one more in the truck—with the dog. He spotted me first, calling out to the others, who didn't want the attention. There was no mistaking their intentions.

They'd found us. They were here to kill us.

"Hey!" I yelled just before they tried the door to our room. With the man in the truck still yelling, they were quick to recognize me. They reached under their jackets for the obvious.

Game on, I thought, knowing how this was going to end.

At least I would die knowing the love of another.

At Elephant Butte Lake, Collette told me she loved me.

Right after I lied to her.

Chapter 40

Foolish, I was.

Usually I had time to plan, to think, to plot, but the men taking aim at me would have none of that. They'd meant to be discreet, but had learned from their associates in Dallas. I was dangerous.

Foolish, I was, to be standing around as a bullet ripped through the window mere inches from my head. Back in Dallas, I was lucky to have the element of surprise, something I'd recklessly sacrificed just now in order to protect Collette.

As I waved my hands again, keeping their attention drawn to me, I thought about it. Perhaps that's what love was—selflessness. Or sheer stupidity, as it was an odd and awful time for my mind to lose focus. If I survived another shot attempt, I could dwell on that later. I ducked and turned to flee, feeling the spark of another bullet as it tore into the concrete at my feet.

Never breaking from my full-on sprint, I weaved my way behind every support column I could. The events of the past few days, as well as today's work, had me mentally in shambles, and my body wasn't any better. Hamstrings strained and tightened as I urged them beyond their capabilities. The safest strategy, besides not letting a bullet rip through my skull, was to head into town, losing them amongst the buildings. But with Collette being a potential target, I couldn't risk someone staying behind at the motel. I needed all of them after me. I could only hope Daniel heard the commotion and would get Collette safely out of there once I was gone.

I hooked a hard right, feeling them closing in on me. Ahead lay a built-up block wall to the rear of the motel. Beyond it lay an open expanse of desert and rocky terrain that might grant me escape, but would also make me an easy target. Rather than hauling ass for it, I suddenly stopped. Anticipating only one of them was in the lead in pursuit, I brought my arm up to deliver a hard swing across my pursuer's throat as he rounded the corner. Before he could slow down or level his handgun to aim, I clotheslined him. He went down hard, banging his head on the ground with a thunk as he left his feet. Definitely a cracked skull. Man was going to need a hospital.

The black Suburban roared through the parking lot, swiftly coming upon us. I picked up his handgun and leveled three quick shots into its windshield. It swerved suddenly, its passengers returning fire as it smacked into a parked Dodge. I wasn't trying for a stand-off; just wanted them to follow me. Taking one more shot over my shoulder, I dashed for the wall. Once I cleared it, I'd be in open space, but with a head start, as they'd have to go around in the truck. My foot bled from the rough, sharp stone barely covered by the sandy topping and loose gravel, but I ignored the pain, focusing instead on my survival.

For a short while, I deluded myself into thinking I would get away. The Suburban hadn't surfaced, and I could see the Mogollon mountain range in Gila National Forest on the horizon, using it as a guide while pressing on in my erratic pattern. I ran hunched over, using any small mounds, crevices, and brush I could to obscure my profile. I came upon an open patch where I would be completely exposed. When I stood up to sprint across, a cloud of dust caught my eye.

It was another black truck. This one was heading toward me in a sweeping pattern from the west. My pursuer must've called them in to cut me off.

I dropped flat, face in the sand, hoping they hadn't spotted me. A scorpion, disturbed from its home, scurried past my face. I held my breath until it was on its way. Free to inhale again, I brought the borrowed gun up from my side and checked it. Only two bullets were left. I adjusted my head enough to see the newest truck. As it moved along, I could see a large brother with dreads, dressed in black, hanging on the exterior, his feet on the step bar and an AK-47 in hand.

It was Loup Garou, Penny Antnee's boy, laughing maniacally as he fired random shots into the countryside. Shit. How serious were they about this thing? Again, it was as if they were two steps ahead of me. I spat out the sand that had accumulated in my mouth and slowly shifted myself around to see behind me. Another cloud of dust was visible and getting closer. I was in a pinch, unable to advance or retreat.

For what felt like an eternity, I lay in the afternoon sun, knowing that as the trucks converged, they'd eventually spot me and kill me. And if they didn't see me, there was the off chance of being run over as they patrolled through the sparse brush. I pretended I was somewhere in a nice air conditioned lounge as I baked, throat burning with each dry swallow. This shit had to end soon.

Loup Garou was close enough to hear. As he reloaded, he teased. "You might as well make it easier on yourself, little rabbit. The more bullets I waste, the more painful I'ma make it for you," the Haitian Werewolf shouted in Creole. Now I could hear the first truck, the Suburban, as it crept into position behind me. Over the growl of its engine, I could make out a growl of another kind.

My options had become more limited. Canine jaws tearing at my throat weren't a pleasant scenario as far as I was concerned. Fuck that. I was born in T or C, but didn't want to die here.

Loup was closest to me, but not for long. Time was up.

I steeled myself for what I had to do, moving my body into position and waiting for Penny's enforcer to begin mouthing off again in frustration.

And he did.

I sprang up from my hiding spot, covered in dirt and sand, startling Loup Garou in mid-sentence. Made him hesitate at the bizarre sight rising like something from beyond the grave. That small delay allowed me to get off the first shot.

The bullet hit him somewhere, knocking him down. I didn't have the luxury of waiting to see where he'd been hit or if he was dead. I was too busy taking the final shot. The driver ducked, thinking he was next. I squeezed the trigger, ridding myself of the final bullet.

It landed exactly where I aimed, blowing out a front tire on the truck. With no use for an empty gun, I let it drop, running for dear life as I headed south. Even if he didn't recognize me from our previous encounters, it was some small satisfaction that I'd slipped away from Loup Garou a third time, however brief it might be.

As I did my best impersonation of a jackrabbit, shots rang out from the Suburban as they'd realized what was happening. They were still too far away to be accurate, but even a lucky shot would do the deed. I moved with the blind hope that there was a road south of here that led back to town.

And that I could somehow outrace a truck full of hired killers.

Chapter 41

Now like a mutha . . . an hour later.

"Amigo, do you need policía?"

"No. Thank you. They're friends of mine. We were playing a game," I deadpanned with a wave of my hand. I was a limping lump of bruises, cuts, and dried blood as I exited the old truck into which I'd jumped to escape. If I were in better shape, I would've had him drop me down the block rather than at the hotel, but walking was a luxury I couldn't afford just yet. I savored the remaining Budweiser he'd given me once safely away from my pursuers, finishing off the can before wiping my cracked lips.

How many times can one cheat death before he flunks the test? Something to ponder later perhaps. For now, I just needed to get to the room and get Collette out of here. Even though they'd let me get away out there in the brush, they could easily have a change in orders that discretion be damned and come back blazing. Daniel saw my drop off and came rushing out his office as I gingerly shuffled by the vacancy sign.

"Madre de dios. What happened to you?" he asked. He looked over me from head to bare, swollen toe, making the sign of the cross quicker than I could blink.

"Water," I requested, handing him the empty beer can in exchange. "Please."

He stared, mouth agape, incredulous at how I looked. Overcoming his need for answers, he complied and ran back inside, quickly returning with not just a bottle of ice cold water, but my cell phone and shoes.

Except for the damaged Dodge on the parking lot whose owners hadn't discovered it yet, the motel seemed eerily business as usual. Like the bizarre display here had been a mirage long faded, except I was evidence of just how real it had been. I downed the bottle of water so fast that it gave me brain freeze. As I confronted the pain, Daniel asked, "Where have you been?"

"Out there," I motioned lazily with my thumb over my shoulder. "Went for a run. Just some crazy stuff. Wait. You didn't see anything?" I asked, surprised.

"No. Sorry. I heard some gunshots, but we get that sometimes. Just coyotes bringing people over from Mexico. I waited for you by the pool and when you didn't return . . . " He shrugged, not fully grasping the severity of what had happened on his grounds. "I have your phone and your shoes. Kept them for you. Safe. Here."

I had Daniel help me sit at the curb. No need walking any further barefooted. Collette was going to smell me regardless and . . .

"Wait, wait, wait," I mumbled, trying to focus through the dull whirring sound in my head as I forced shoes on swollen feet. "You didn't go by the room?"

"No," he replied. "When you didn't return, I thought . . . Well, *you two are young.* I figured you would come get me when you were 'done,' so I returned to my office and the air conditioning," he admitted with a sheepish grin.

I tried to stand too fast. Daniel had to assist me yet again, but I quickly pushed off to get a painful trajectory going that would take me directly across the parking lot to our room.

"Please, please. Please be there," I pled faintly, afraid that if my fears were spoken too loudly that they would manifest as punishment for my multitude of sins. I needed Collette to greet me with that smile, to innocently chastise me for taking all day, and ask me how the pool looked. I needed her to take me in her arms, despite my current state. To cradle me and tell me it all would be okay.

A few doors down, the cleaning lady was knocking to provide room service. One more stop and she would see the bullet hole left in the vacant room's window or the shell casings scattered here and there. When the hidden signs were revealed or when my pursuers returned, all hell was going to break loose. I tried to retrieve my key, but must've lost it somewhere in the barren expanse round back.

"I have a another key," Daniel said as he trailed me, ready to render assistance if I should fall over, but also seeking complete answers as to what happened to me.

"It's okay," I said, trying to get him to return to the office. My act was a flimsy one as every syllable still stung, my throat burning in retaliation for my daring to communicate. As I resumed my mission, I found myself chilled to the bone despite the oppressive heat. Fresh streaks of crimson were present on the walkway outside our room. My remaining adrenaline kicking in, I limped as fast as I could, bashing the door open in frantic desperation.

"Collette!" I screamed, wincing immediately from the pain. Collette wouldn't be cradling me or chastising me for she was nowhere to be seen. In her stead was a room that had been decimated. It didn't take much of an imagination to figure out how valiantly she'd fought despite her disability. But her reward for that struggle was evident by the blood soaked comforter I'd bought for her.

So much blood.

"No! No!" I screamed, crumpling onto my knees. I clawed at my face, sobbing uncontrollably before erupting in a primal scream contained only by my strained vocal cords. Housekeeping came over to see what the commotion was about, but Daniel cursed at her in Spanish to move on. He shook me, coaxing me away from the despair threatening to engulf me all the while horrified by what he witnessed.

I'd never see Collette again. They'd taken away the only real thing that meant something to me. I knew how people like this operated. Either her body would never be found or it would conveniently surface in connection with me. It was never more evident how utterly powerless I was. No need for them to return. In spite of my miraculous escape, they'd gotten me. I was broken, tumbling in freefall as my mind fractured until Daniel shook me.

"Don't know what is going on, but you must leave now!" he commanded.

"They . . . they think I kidnapped her," I babbled, but I was . . . trying to protect her. I . . ." I wept openly before Daniel.

"Hush. I know you didn't kidnap that woman. I wouldn't have let you stay if I thought you had," he offered, admitting for the first time that he'd seen something about Collette's disappearance on the news. "But you must leave now and never come back. This is a small town and people talk. Especially the help."

"She didn't deserve this," I said, my hands trembling uncontrollably.

"Don't do this to yourself. She wouldn't want it this way. You must know that."

More of the cleaning staff had gathered, word spreading of what was unfolding at the motel. Too many people looking at my exposed face, scoured free of all masks by the day's events.

"Thank you, Daniel," I said for a final time, shaking his hand. I straightened up; tried to hold my head high for the onlookers that had accumulated as I morphed into another role, that of a survivor, as best I could under the circumstances.

"Adios, my friend. Try to be well. Do it for her," he offered. "Be sure to tell your madre what I did for you today."

"My mother's dead. Been dead," I finally admitted as I walked away.

And now so was I.

I'd slept for days, having checked in under another of my assumed names. The bandages I'd used to cover my injuries and obscure my face were discarded. Rather than exploring Glendale, Arizona, I'd stayed in, ordering room service sparingly just to regain some strength. The body would heal, but I was wounded far beyond that. The TV had remained off as my mind drifted back and forth; torn between grand mayhem and the deliverance of suicide as I stared up at the textured ceiling.

My cell phone rang, temporarily halting my pathetic debate. I looked at the number then answered.

"Hello."

"Hey, I got the whereabouts of that Sophia girl you were asking about," Dom Fuentes, the parole agent from California stated. "We're straight after this, right?"

"Yeah, we're done," I replied, an eerie calmness sweeping over me. Suicide could wait a little longer.

Chapter 42

I watched her car through the window as she drove up. While she shopped, I'd gone through the house, ensuring she had no roommates or other surprises that might pop up. Dimming the lights, I waited for her to come in. I'd easily bypassed the simple little tricks and traps she used to tell if somebody had intruded. The door unlocked, proving me right.

Upon entering, Sophia set down her purse and shopping bags. Just as she realized the lights were out where she'd left them on, it was too late. I shut the door behind her.

"Knew you'd miss me," she said, noticing her purse, with whatever protection it held, was suddenly gone.

"You fucked me," I said as I came up behind her, placing the barrel of the gun at the base of her skull.

"Yeah. And it was good, huh?"

"No. You *really* fucked me," I said, pressing the barrel harder. "Why here?"

"You said to disappear, so I picked this place. As good as any. Rent's cheap."

"Stockton? You live for the thrill. This ain't a thrill."

"Got another reason for me being here?" she challenged.

"Yes, I do. Mule Creek," I answered, referring to the California state prison she'd been visiting regularly in nearby Ione. I rattled her. Could tell from the way her neck tensed beneath the barrel.

"Never heard of it," she said as calmly as she could. That's why I stayed behind her. I didn't want to look in the eyes of such a master, someone who could generate a variety of conflicting emotions in me while preying on all of them.

"That is why you're here, right? Waiting for him to be released? Waiting for him to come strolling out next week and sweep you up in his arms? Fairy tale sound about right? *Do I still make you cum harder than him*?" I taunted, recalling her admission back in Vegas.

"I . . . don't know what you're talking about. Have you been drinking, Truth?"

"Nah. I'm sober, Sophia. So when I say you're not going to see him walk out of prison, I mean it. At least . . . not out the front gate. He's dead.

Killed last night. And from what I know, it was pretty painful."

"You're lying," she said, whipping around recklessly. I held the gun, still pointed at her, resisting the urge to drop her on the spot. It was hard not to because I kept seeing Collette's face, all that blood everywhere. "You don't know anything about him."

"Ivan Dempsey's his name, right? Crackhead former model? I'm sure they *loved him long time* on the inside. Maybe I'm lying. Maybe he's not dead. Or maybe . . . just maybe I can see into the future. He's not being released anytime soon. Seems he's misbehaved and is being transferred to another facility. And if you try to reach him, try to see him or have any contact ever again, I will find out, and my vision of the future becomes a reality."

"Why are you doing this to me?" she asked, erupting in a fit of sorrow and rage. Losing him meant more to her than her own sad life. I knew how she felt.

Flaring up, I put one in the chamber, sending her scrambling backward in a panic. She fell down as I advanced, knocking over a glass table. She brought her hands up over her face as she shrieked.

"You're lucky I don't just kill you, but you're not worth the cost of the bullet," I snarled, standing over her. "Consider this payback for what you took from me."

"What the fuck are you talking about?" she sobbed, her hands trembling and eyes bulging.

"All I did was swipe stuff off your computer, man! What other issues you have, don't you dare lay them on me!"

"Don't fuck with me, Sophia!" I yelled, wagging the gun at her. "You know you sicced Penny Antnee and them on me with those pictures! I hope you got enough money for that! Or did it give you satisfaction because I chose Collette over you? Huh? Well, now your cousin's dead because of it!"

"Dead? Collette? Wow." Sophia chuckled inappropriately. She mused over my news, seeming to forget the gun pointed at her head. "Are you sure?" she asked, her pitch oddly rising.

"Yes, they killed her! And you want to laugh about it? What's your game, you sick, twisted bitch?"

"No game. I just appreciate irony." She sighed. "Penny Antnee didn't pay me. Collette did."

"What?"

"She's not my cousin, Truth. We're not related at all. She paid me to get close to you, you jackass!"

Sophia flipped a switch, causing a chain reaction of past events cascading through my mind.

"What you got to say now?" She smirked in as defiant a manner as I'd ever seen.

I replied by unloading the .45 until the clip was empty.

Chapter 43

With cash on hand from one of my accounts and another laptop, I was back in business with a reach that knew no bounds. With the issue of Sophia resolved and free of Collette's influence, I was locked on a singular priority—payback.

In a coffee shop similar to one I'd shared with Collette in days now gone, I scoured the Internet for any unreported, unsubstantiated rumors from the entertainment world. The aroma of the fresh ground beans didn't escape me. I imagined that awful blend I used to order simply to bond with her. Yet somehow I found myself longing for its taste.

Spin was in full effect. 4Shizzle had put its simmering exposé on me on hold, instead posting a blind item about a Florida rapper, obviously referring to Loup Garou, being shot in some rap feud. Shot, but not dead. The front of a "rap feud" be damned; I only hated that the fucker still walked the Earth. Despite Sophia's revelations about Collette, her absence hurt worse than anything I'd ever been through. With each passing day, that frigid chasm inside me grew. The only thing keeping the chill at bay was the white hot rage I felt for Loup Garou. I feared the depression that was to come once this was over. I remembered the despair that tore apart my mother after Hollywood. Was this what was inevitable after losing all one cared for?

Knowing the story being put out about Loup Garou, I began working contacts both near and far—a police officer who moonlighted as security in L.A., a woman in airline reservations for Continental, a parking lot attendant whose sister has a kid by someone in the music industry, a limo driver, a VIP concierge for American Express, and last but not least, a drug dealer with contacts throughout south Florida. With the most trivial and anecdotal evidence gathered, I sifted through the bullshit, piecing together an educated guess of where he was holed up.

The north side of Las Vegas. At a home leased by Penny Antnee's talent agency.

I figured him as wanting to return to the cradle. Back to Miami, his stomping grounds, where family protected him and he could recover in peace. Would've made it much harder to find him, more dangerous, too but apparently he didn't fear the

man who'd shot him. Although I could be a rabbit
if the situation called for it, he was about to have
the rabbit turn and bite him.

I smiled as I booked my flight, knowing retri-
bution was in order, whether I lived through it
or not.

"You sure they're for us?" the red-eyed hang-
er-on asked, marijuana smoke evident in the
air as he hung from the open door. Unlike my
previous encounter with Penny's people, the tall,
gangly man posed no threat.

The hired guns used in Dallas and back in T or
C were still unsuccessfully combing the country
for me, but Loup Garou chose to convalesce with
his boys and the regular entourage while Penny
Antnee did his mega-star thing. My guess was
that Loup Garou was the only one in the posse
privy to his boy's indiscretions or the lengths
he'd go to silence people over it. For all the rest
knew, Loup Garou really had been shot in some
feud.

"Hey, my man," I chimed in the nasally voice
I'd rehearsed all day. "I just do as I'm told. I get
paid either way, knowhutI'msayin'?"

"Who sent em?" he asked, leering at the volup-
tuous working girls I'd rounded up from around

the city. I'd paid them cash up front, with the
agreement that all tips were theirs with no split.
Only one of them knew I was not what I seemed.

"You know I don't talk," I replied with a smile
and a wink from behind my dark sunglasses.
"Not only do people take care of Penny, they also
take care of his peeps."

"Whoa. That's what's up." He chuckled as he
rubbed his hands together briskly.

"Now, can we come in?" I asked, gesturing
wildly in my black tailored suit while steady
smacking my worn chewing gum. "'Cause I don't
think the neighbors would appreciate what these
girls here are about ta do."

"Right, right. Get yo' asses on in here then," he
urged with glee.

I spat out my gum then held the door open,
gentleman-like, as the seven ladies entered. The
fool was so fixated on the women that he didn't
bother to frisk me. A raucous roar erupted in
the house as news spread of the visitors. Before
things got out of hand, I held audience in the living room with the men, informing them of what
they could and could not do. My instructions
served dual purposes—to pretend I was really
the girls' handler, and to get a head count of the
house. When I was done, it was time to play.

"How do you want to do it?" the dancer called Fierce whispered to me as the festivities kicked off.

"When things go south, just say you saw somebody go out the back door. You remember the description?"

"Yeah, yeah. You drilled it into me," she answered.

Before long, the boys remembered to be considerate to the ailing. Fierce was the one who volunteered to play Florence Nightingale. I watched where she went in the house, all the while playing bored sitter.

"Say, man, I'm going to take a smoke. Call my wife," I rattled off to the closest person coherent enough to care, motioning as if the loud music might hinder my conversation. "Behave with the ladies, okay?"

I opened the back door, walking onto the patio for the briefest of seconds before reentering and heading straight for one of the bedrooms.

"What the—?"

I cut off Loup Garou's exclamation with a wave of the silencer-tipped gun in my gloved hand. "Wait outside the door," I calmly instructed Fierce.

"Who the fuck are you, man?" Loup groaned as Fierce left us alone. "I was about to get my dick sucked." I got to see my desert handiwork, a bit of white gauze and tape on the upper part of his chest, near his shoulder. A little lower and to the left and I would've had his heart. Several bottles of antibiotics and pain pills rested on the tray next to his bed. Despite his weariness, he tried to keep his thug on for appearance's sake.

"Look at my face," I said, coming closer.

"I've been shot. Don't feel so good. Man, go on with that shit," he said, waving me away as if I were a minor inconvenience.

"I'm not in a caring mood. Look closely."

He indulged me, looking once then looking away before quickly looking again. His groggy eyes flashed with brilliance. "That was you in New Mexico. You's a quick motherfucker. Shoulda had yo' ass."

"And out here at the hotel Stratus that time, when you were following me and I got you popped by the cops. And in Houston."

"Houston?"

"At that lounge. When the guy was messing with Natalia and he said I paid him to do it. I was the guy with the fiancée," I said, making a poor attempt at faux eyeglasses with my free hand.

"You a real fuckin' Eddie Murphy or somethin' with the disguises 'n shit. But why you tellin' me?"

"Maybe I just need to feel appreciated."

"Maybe you here to pop me for what I done to ya."

"No. That's was just business. I put myself in *a position to get caught slippin'*," I clowned with an ill attempt at rhyme. "You just took advantage of it. I'm here for the bonus shit."

The Haitian Werewolf grinned, his gold fang fronts absent for a change. He looked away, taking a heavy, labored breath. "Go ahead. I ain't gonna scream. I ain't no bitch," he grunted.

"Can I ask you something? Before I—"

"Shoot," he said, irony intended.

"Why do all this for Penny?"

"Boy got talent by the pound. Can't let shit happen to him or his career, y'know. He takes care of a lot of people. Been rollin' wit' him since way back."

"You and him . . . ?"

"Nah. That's my boy though. I love him, but not like that." Loup broke down for the briefest of seconds, realizing the love he had for his boy Penny wasn't going to get him through the night. "Man, fuck the civilians. Shouldn't have let you get away in New Mexico."

There was a thump as something fell over in another room. The party was escalating, heading to its natural conclusion. I'd kept Fierce waiting outside the door too long already. Somebody would eventually pass down the hallway.

"Give me closure, Werewolf. What did you do with her body?"

He stared at me, not giving up anything beyond a sly smile. "Little rabbit, you didn't come here to talk, no?" he taunted with as much diminished swagger as he could conjure up.

I counted off two seconds, giving him the briefest of chances to reconsider and answer.

"No," I replied, as I put a single bullet between his cold eyes.

Chapter 44

I pulled my trench coat tight as I moved with the foot traffic down West Thirty-third. The Knicks were set to lose another one at MSG tonight, and the weather reminded me why I didn't live here, despite my love for New Yorkers. Had to appreciate their brutal honesty in a world full of spineless liars. I jaywalked across the street over to One Penn Plaza, darting under the construction scaffolding and through the entrance as renovations took place.

I entered the FedEx Office, milling amongst the Manhattanites as I searched for a certain someone. A cute young thang with "Smart" on her nametag zigged and zagged around store displays and supplies, oblivious to the customers as others attended to them. Kinda young for store manager, but there it was on the eyeglass wearer's tag.

"Excuse me, ma'am," a man offered in a broken English dialect as she tried to hurry by. She held up a sole finger, indicating that she was speaking on her headset. Cute that no one here knew her true nature, possessing a façade like so many of mine.

"Sir, just take a place in line and someone will be right with you." Although different in tone, her voice was unmistakable as that with which I'd conversed once before—when I'd begged her to back off.

"Just need a moment of your time, miss. I need to know if your store provides this service," the elderly man said as he unfolded a tiny slip of paper and handed it to her. Lorelei Smart, the MIT dropout from the Jacob Riis projects on the lower East Side, read the single phrase: *4Shizzle*. I watched her jaw tighten as her engineer's mind tried to anticipate three steps ahead.

"I don't know what this is," she lied. "Sir, this . . . is . . . a . . . FedEx Office." She spoke deliberately for the man's benefit. She handed the paper back to him, ensuring it looked like a common mistake to her customers. The nice gentleman departed the store having done his part. And all it took from me was a cup of coffee and a bagel from the Dunkin Donuts in the same building.

I'd watched it all, observing the observant, four steps ahead of her three. When she retreated to the manager's office in back, I was already seated at the powerful computer she used for much more than "your shipping or business needs."

"Hi," I said with a grin. "Why don't you have a seat?" I offered just as I cracked her computer password, her mother's name with numbers substituted for the vowels. She wasn't the first person whose ego made them sloppy on their turf. "What's the scoop today? Some star popped with a DWI? No, wait. Somebody's register came up short on last night's shift. Or are you two reams short on copier paper?"

"Sir, we don't allow customers back here. I'm about to call the police," the editor of 4Shizzle said straight-faced, still playing her role. She'd done so well hiding her true identity behind the older, wise-cracking, sexy online persona she'd cultivated. Yet here I was, staring down the real item.

"Why? Lorelei, you offered to make me famous. Remember? Or was that just when you were safe behind your screen name 'n shit? I'm here to make you famous instead. No instant messaging or all that stuff. No tweets. Face to face. You get the exclusive today . . . if you don't pee on yourself first."

"I ain't afraid of you," she snorted, trying to convince one of us in the tiny room.

"Maybe you should be these days. Things haven't been going so good for me, thanks in no small part to you. Killing Loup Garou has gone a long way toward calming my nerves, so that's a good thing . . . for you."

"Oh my gawd," Lorelei gasped. My joke about her peeing on herself almost came true. "You're making that up to scare me. They said it was a gang hit. Finishing what they started."

I chuckled. "Hope you didn't pay them for that story."

Her reflexes probably screamed at her to run, but she indulged me. I figured her greed for the scoop would override her fears. "You're lying," she pushed.

"Wouldn't you prefer the truth? Or are you comfortable going with what they're feeding you? I thought 4Shizzle prided itself on the truth."

"Lor, you in there?" her co-worker called through the door. "Juan gotta leave early. Again."

"Your decision," I mouthed softly. She had a clear shot to run for it and risk that I was telling the truth about not being here to kill her.

"I'm on a conference call. Get someone else to cover for him," she shouted back, making her choice.

"Okay, but that's some bullshit," the co-worker griped, ending their dialogue with her and storming back to the front.

"Just another day, huh?" I said while browsing through her files. I smiled, recognizing a few random tidbits courtesy of me, and seeing who were some of her other sources.

"You wanna get away from my computer?"

"Touchy. I used to be like that with mine. Before it took a bullet meant for me. Does your mother know about your real career?"

"No. That's why I do this shit. It was hard enough getting her to let me come home after I skipped college. Wait. How did you—"

"After all this time, do you have to ask?" What we didn't get into was how Lorelei used most of her earnings from 4Shizzle to pay for her mother's cancer treatment and support her crackhead sister with three kids in Jersey. That rare bit of goodness and her being just a kid herself spared Lorelei the fate of so many others who'd crossed me.

"I got work to get back to. What is it you want to tell me?" She sighed.

"Everything," I offered as I gave up the chair in front of her prized repository of scandal. "Wanna cue the Usher music? 'Cause these are my confessions."

I talked while 4Shizzle's enigmatic editor listened, filling her in on the back story behind so much of the dirt I'd funneled her way. Every time she tried to type or write down what I was saying, I would stop her, leaving her to fidget nervously in her chair.

"How much do you want for all this?" she asked, sitting still for the first time and shifting back into the business mode of a person older than what she was.

"Nothing. I just figured I'd give you as much as I reasonably could and let you make up your mind about getting dragged down where I'm at right now."

"Why do I get the feeling I'm never going to hear from you again?"

"Don't fight that feeling, Ms. Smart. Is this more than you bargained for?"

"Yeah," the young girl answered solemnly. "She didn't tell me all this about you."

"Because Sophia didn't know me long enough to tell you."

"Who?"

"The person who gave you those unedited photos of Penny Antnee and Andre Martin."

"That wasn't her name."

"I didn't expect her to use her real name with you."

"No. That wasn't her name at all. I ain't dumb. I can find out things too, y'know."

"Then who was it?" I barked, dreading what she might say.

"Shit. What's her name?" she cursed to herself, fumbling with her thoughts. "That one they accuse you of kidnapping."

"Collette."

"Yeah! That's it!"

"*She gave you those photos*?"

"Yeah. We spoke on the phone and then I got the e-mail. So?"

"Maybe . . . maybe Sophia put her up to it," I tried to reason with myself as I began pacing. "Doesn't matter anyway. She's dead now. That's why I killed Loup Garou."

"Okay, this shit is getting too crazy for me now. You need to leave before I get fired. Please."

"What's wrong?" I asked. "You're hiding something."

"C'mon, can you please leave already?" she pleaded.

"Are you really going to make me go back on my promise?" I threatened, fed up with the bullshit I'd been through.

"All right! All right! I don't want to die. Sheesh. I'll tell you," she yelped, exiting her chair and heading toward the door. In a frantic huff, she opened it before turning back toward me.

Lorelei's lip trembled. "That girl. Collette."

"Yeah? What?"

"She called me yesterday," she whispered, almost embarrassed. "She's not dead, man."

I held the chair to steady myself as Lorelei darted out the door, leaving me alone in her office.

Alone as the walls closed in.

OMG, I would've typed if communicating over our usual medium.

Chapter 45

I came back.

One mo' gain.

Back to T or C, the town that birthed me and the desert that almost claimed me.

Maybe I should've let it be. The dramatic turn of events had me at wit's end. My last time here, I was off my game. Delirious flights of fancy had me not seeing the next move until it had occurred. I'd operated so long in lies that maybe the field had caught up with me. Like a typical old man being caught up in a young man's game, waking up one day and realizing that there just *might* be someone out there better—fuck that—*maybe almost as good* as you.

Despite what I'd heard in New York, I had to see things yet again, but with eyes wide open. Needed to focus on the chessboard without benefit of forked tongue in my ear or pussy on the brain. I stood there in the cool early morning on the parking lot of the Asilo Rojo Inn, and although I dreaded replaying that critical time, I did what I had to do. I walked outside the door of the room we'd shared, imagining all the blood I saw. Remembered the streaks on the ground and the pain I felt when I thought Collette was lost to me.

Then I rewound back to when that particular day began, skipping past the mad dash for my life. Back to when Daniel asked me to assist him with the pool. I remembered his dreams of how he wanted kids frolicking in it while their parents looked on. From where I stood, I could see the yellow tape was absent from it. I walked closer, still unnoticed. The repairs to the pool were almost complete, its rehabilitation a reality. *Just add water*, it advertised. Impressive for such a short period of time and on the limited budget Daniel professed to have.

If Daniel was around, there were none of the normal indicators. A brand new truck sat where his old beat-up one was usually parked, suggesting change was afoot. That and the pool answered a lot for me. Either someone new had taken over the motel, or I was headed for a reckoning. I walked briskly, prepared to confront either.

As I entered the office, the bell rang. Daniel was busy on the phone, arguing in Spanish about the new sign that was to have been delivered yesterday. When he turned around to greet me, we made eye contact. He froze before hanging up, ending his argument abruptly. I rewound back to when I found Collette suspiciously talking to him at this very spot. She was negotiating with him.

He is not so blind who cannot see, but who refuses to see.

"Damn. She paid you well," I commented, seeing it all laid out before me.

I'd barely uttered the words before Daniel reached for a shotgun from behind the counter and drew it on me, reflexes faster than I'd guessed. Adrenaline or sheer fear will do that though.

"I told you not to come back, amigo," he hissed nervously. I reflected on the seemingly innocent conversation he was having with Collette when I walked in on them. Remembered how Penny's boys happened to arrive while Daniel had me occupied. Remembered his desperate insistence that I get out of here when I found the bloodied, trashed room minus Collette.

As calm and pristine as things were now, you'd think all that was a figment of my imagination. Except the gun barrel pointed at my center mass was a friendly dose of reality to remind me that I wasn't wrong about all this.

My phone rang and Daniel flinched. I showed it to him and slowly raised it to my ear. Careful not to have Daniel mess up his lobby with parts of me just yet. I'd put all my contacts into play before boarding the plane from New York, and one of them was calling me to report in.

"Did you find her?" I asked loudly for Daniel's benefit. He'd begun sweating, and the barrel of the gun wobbled ever so slightly. Somehow that made me calmer.

"Yeah. And it wasn't hard either," the boisterous hairdresser in Allen, Texas, a northern suburb of Dallas, replied on the other end of the phone. "You still owe me the agreed upon amount, right?"

"Yes," I replied with a sigh. My life was in jeopardy again, so quibbling over money was a low priority. "Where is she?"

"Here," she replied. "She's on all the channels. You watching?"

"I'll have to call you back," I said. Daniel had lowered his aim to wipe the sweat off his forehead, his eyes twitching now. He made the sign of the cross as I hung up. "You might need that divine intervention; especially if you miss your shot," I said to him, aiming an empty finger at him with a smile and gesturing as if it were a gun of my own.

He looked puzzled for a moment by my gall before focusing on his aim, preparing to match my imaginary shot with one of more substance. If Collette had just surfaced like my caller said, I was probably confirmed as her kidnapper. Daniel would be the hero, having taken out the big bad man. Maybe even reap more than whatever he'd been paid by Collette to manipulate me during our stay.

Checkmate on my ass.

Daniel was sweating more profusely now. I took a deep breath, but refused to close my eyes as he squinted to get off a good shot. Just as his finger squeezed the trigger, he seized up, suddenly gasping. The shotgun rang out, peppering the lobby wall two feet to my left, a stray pellet hitting me in my arm. Daniel dropped the gun, gripping his chest in agony.

The divine intervention was on my behalf.

"My . . . heart. I need my pills," he wheezed as he tried to brace himself on the counter. "They . . . they're over there. Por favor."

"And you want me to get them?" I pondered.

"*Sí, sí.* You're Leila's son. I loved her. I . . . I wasn't going to shoot you."

"Could've fooled me," I said, coming around the counter to kick his shotgun farther beyond his reach. He tried to clutch my arm, but I backed away. When he tumbled onto the floor, I watched him for a moment, listening to his groans until they ceased. My mother's soap opera lover and Jason—the rare potential father figures I'd had in my life—had all been major disappointments. Daniel was no different.

I left the Asilo Rojo Inn and its foolish old proprietor, free of any childhood delusions that held me back, for the small town held neither truth nor consequences for me.

Chapter 46

Arriving back in Dallas, it was all over the news, just as my informant had said. Rather than wire transfers, she preferred cold, hard cash, so I delivered her finder's fee to her Mail Boxes Etc. location as requested.

As far as the media story spun, the poor blind girl who'd been kidnapped had surfaced alive, much to the Metroplex's joy. A great big Texas-sized "Yee-haw" was called for. But every good fairy tale needs a monster.

A friend named Chris Davis, who Collette thought was a good, kind man, became more belligerent and unstable as time went on. This worried Collette, even scared her. She tried calling it off, but he refused, threatening her with bodily harm if she did. After breaking in her apartment and trashing the place, he kidnapped her, holding her for days at a place she couldn't identify. When he left her alone for a moment, she ran for it, succeeding in hitchhiking back home, where she notified the authorities. She was lucky enough to escape with her life, especially since this same person was wanted in connection with the murder of a businessman in the elevator of his apartment complex.

Someone had provided a sketch that was a pretty good likeness of me, too, so law enforcement was asking for leads. I'll be damned. After years of operating in the shadows, I'd made Crime Stoppers. That meant I had to operate around Dallas, the one place I was becoming comfortable as myself, in one of many guises.

No matter, for am I not Proteus, wearer of many forms?

I say that as if I weren't wounded by Collette, but I was. Emotions were my enemy, and had gained the upper hand throughout this entire escapade. Probably from day one, when I was stupid enough to get too close to her. Now, like the moth drawn to the flame, I had to enter it. Face whatever was there.

And see if my wings were fireproof.

After the initial interviews and meeting with the detectives, Collette claimed to simply want her privacy back, and retreated from the public view. She never even gave them my real name, nor mentioned New Mexico. Too many questions, and she was bound to give the wrong answer eventually, which might poke holes in her tale. As well as she'd done me, she still wasn't a pro.

Due to her disability and the media attention, Dallas PD assigned someone to look after her, as I was still on the loose. Despite my anger and conflicted feelings of love and betrayal, I waited patiently over the next several weeks before getting a message in Braille into Collette's hands.

That was the easy part.

The difficult part was figuring which buttons to push on the woman I thought I knew, without winding up on death row for a murder that ironically was self-defense.

For all the wrong I'd done, it would be fitting.

I waited in Bob Jones Park in Southlake, a small town northwest of Dallas, after dark. Saw the lights of the taxi cab as it drove slowly down the wooded trail, the driver no doubt listening to Collette's instructions and wondering if she were crazy. They'd driven from the developed portion of land onto what was essentially a nature preserve. One with only a bare minimum of signage visible for the hikers that ventured out this way.

The cab came to a stop. I could hear the loud voice of the cabbie, probably warning her against getting out . . . especially in her condition. She ignored him and exited the cab, a plume of faint road dust hovering before its headlights.

"Truth, are you here?" she called out. She wore a light-colored sweater and jeans, looking just as beautiful I recalled. A woman I would have died for, now wanting me to meet that very end.

"Yes," I answered, stepping from out the brush, where I'd been waiting for hours, never quite sure if she would show. The park was named for a freed slave, and heaven knows a slave could hide in here without being found if he chose. If this was a setup on Collette's part, further betrayal not out of the question, I might have a chance to be that rabbit once again, like I was in T or C.

Still inside his car, and with the engine running, the cabbie probably didn't hear me answer. Collette leaned into the open door, thanking him before she shut it. Still not fully exposing myself, I watched her open her collapsible white cane with that customary snap I'd come to know. Fully extended, it seemed to glow by the eerie starlight overhead tonight. Afraid to drive further into the woods, the cabbie instead backed up to return from whence he came.

Besides my location, my instructions in Braille were to have the cab leave for thirty minutes before coming back for her. She'd followed them up to this point, so maybe some trust still existed. With the cab sufficiently backed away, I approached her. My night vision was returning after the bright headlights disappeared.

"Didn't know if you'd come," I said with a pause, briefly imagining the joy I'd felt back when the two of us were together alone at Elephant Butte back in T or C. I wanted to reach out and take her hand; to put it to my face and introduce myself to her again.

To start anew.

Hi, my name is Truth, and there's a long story behind it. What's yours?

"Why this place?" she asked, swatting at a bug that had landed on her. A large airliner from DFW Airport flew overhead, its engines roaring as it climbed to the heavens.

"Good fishing," I joked. In a move she couldn't have anticipated, I removed a revolver from under my bright red jacket. "Here. I have a gun. Catch, it's loaded" I said, pitching it underhanded toward her on a hunch.

By starlight, I watched her panic as the notion of it accidentally going off surely ran through her head. She let go of her walking stick. I watched her face track the wayward motion of the heavy object tossed to her.

Then I watched her catch it in both hands, cradling it before bringing it into her body. Much like San Antonio Jackson or Andre Martin would do with a football if either still had a future in the NFL.

She could see.

The final betrayal, one I didn't want to believe despite all I'd learned up to this point.

Collette could fucking see.

"Damn," I muttered, wanting anything but the truth right now. "You . . . you lied to me."

"Rather funny coming from you," she spat, staring me down with unyielding eyes. She righted the revolver, taking aim dead. Even in the dark, the bright red of my jacket was a tempting bull's-eye in the remaining field of black I wore.

"Is that why you lied to the police? Wanted to kill me yourself? That is what you want to do, right? That's why I brought the gun for you. I lied to you. Betrayed you. Now you can finish it."

"And . . . you . . . deserve . . . to . . . die, you bastard!" Collette said, baring her teeth as she bordered on hyperventilating. "You took away the one person in the world that meant something to me!"

"I'm sorry for that, Collette," I said, pained as I came to realize that despite the momentary fantasy of the past few months, I never had a chance. As angered as I'd been up to this point, the fact that she wanted me dead no longer mattered.

"No, you're not. Don't ever say that!" I heard the hammer click back as Collette prepared to exact her revenge.

"How'd you know? At least tell me that."

"Your voice. I'll never forget your voice. It's like a bell ringing in my head every time you speak. You were there when it happened. You were there when Myron blew himself up. You knew. You . . . killed . . . my husband!"

"He did it to himself, Collette. He was cheating on you. I . . . didn't know he'd—"

"Blow himself up and try to kill me too? What kind of monster are you?"

One that loves you no matter what you think of me."

"Love? Is that what made you fuck Sophia? *Love for me?*" Collette shot at my feet, clearly coming to terms with what she was going to do. "It sickened me to do the things I did with you. Don't you dare talk to me about love!"

"How long have you been able to see? It couldn't have been this entire time. I saw you. I saw your hospital records."

"Long enough. It was gradual. Long enough to see your lying face all those times in the bookstore."

"And you never said anything. Hell, you even slept with me. You kept up this charade for what? For revenge?"

"Hell yes. Wouldn't you? Besides, I wasn't one hundred percent certain the voice I heard was yours. Not until he told me."

"Who?" I asked, dumbfounded.

"A man," she replied, sniffling. "I don't know his name. He told me everything about you. Told me how you'd set up Myron. Said you were a manipulator and a liar and that I should be careful ."

"And this led you to set all this up? A stranger? To have Sophia get inside my head then steal from me? To make me think you were dead too? Did you know what that did to me?"

"Fuck you! I wanted to hurt you because you deserve to be hurt! To die on the inside just like I had! You took more from me than my sight, Truth! You are the devil, and there's no cost that I'm not willing to pay!" she screamed, waving the gun at me for emphasis. Distraught, she'd crossed that line, a line I was used to, having pushed many people over it in my life. There was no going back. Only one of us would be leaving here tonight.

"Collette, in spite of all this, I know some part of you loves me too. I do. But I don't blame you for what you must do. I just wanted to make up for things somehow." I closed my eyes, realizing that she was right.

I didn't know how to love.

"He said you were good at getting inside people's heads. And not to let you," she rambled. She wiped her eyes again, quickly resuming her aim. I wasn't going anywhere. I owed this much to her.

"Who is this man you keep talking about?"

"I told you I don't know his name. He approached me one day after you started coming around. I never saw him again, until that day back in New Mexico. You were watching him on TV while I pretended to be asleep. I recognized him then. He was talking about Penny Antnee and signing him."

Jason. He'd betrayed me eight ways till Sunday.

And he'd have the last laugh with me out of the way.

"That man was right to warn you about me. I played with you because I could," I muttered, giving Collette what she needed rather than what I needed. "Let's get this over with. Do it! Pull the fucking trigger!" I urged.

Collette aimed again as I held my breath, readying myself. But try as she may, she couldn't do it. She was as conflicted as I. I slowly extended my hand to tell her it was all right. Despite what I'd put her through, she wasn't a killer. But I had become one for her, wrongfully thinking myself her avenging angel.

Words were forming in my mouth when a shot rang out. It struck me in the chest, rupturing the fabric of my jacket and dropping me to my knees in searing pain.

As I struggled to breathe, unable to recover, another person joined us. He was walking down the dirt trail taken by the cab earlier, his freshly discharged gun still centered on me. She hadn't lost the Dallas PD cop assigned to watch over her.

He took another shot, knocking me into the dirt. I blanked out for a second, coming to in more searing agony than before and wishing I were already dead.

It was the police officer who'd taken the report of her break-in that day. I tried to will myself to move, hunching up on my arms as I tried to drag myself to safety.

"No!" Collette screamed, second thoughts I imagine at seeing her darkest desire fulfilled. I took some solace in that as I absorbed a brutal kick in my side that sent me rolling over. Spitting up dirt, I looked into the officer's eyes as he stood over me.

"Thank you," I said, wheezing and gasping to get the words out for my executioner. That was just before he took a final shot at point blank range then, with his foot, rolled me over into the shallow, damp drop-off just within the woodline.

As the two forms standing above me darkened, went blurry then faded away, my last thought was about how proud my mom would have been.

My command performance.

Cue the applause as the curtain closes.

Good-bye, Collette. I hope I've given you in death what I couldn't give you in life: closure.

Chapter 47

"Wake up," he said for the second time as he slapped my face. As my eyes focused, I expected to see perhaps what the devil looked like. Instead, I saw the man who'd just shot me.

Repeatedly.

The sun was coming up over his shoulder, giving him an unlikely halo.

I tried to speak, unaware of how long I'd been unconscious or how badly I'd been hurt. I could taste the dried blood in my mouth. Officer Kane got me to sit up and gave me an ice cold bottled water from his backpack. I tried to drink too fast and wound up choking and spitting up.

"Easy, easy," he said as I cleared my parched throat of the excess water. I was surprised he'd returned. As thorough as he'd been, I very well could have died if left out here alone much longer.

"Is . . . she?"

"Yeah. She's back home, man. Couldn't come back sooner because she was too torn up over all this."

"Torn up? Over me?"

"Well . . . maybe," he reluctantly admitted. "But she's okay with it now."

"What . . . did . . . you tell her?" I inquired, wincing in pain with each breath.

"That I needed to go back and dispose of the body. Make sure you weren't found. I told her it was for her own good, which is why I pulled the trigger when she couldn't."

"You like her, don't you?" I said, forcing a smile as he removed the bright red jacket I wore, exposing the Kevlar vest beneath. I was sure to have a few broken ribs, especially from that last shot he took to my sternum.

"Yeah. I'm feelin' her style."

"How could you not? She's special. In spite of the mess I've put her through."

"You still sure about all this?" he asked while assisting me with the removal of my vest. While it was bulletproof, I certainly wasn't. I grimaced as it separated from my tender skin. Deep, deep bruises were evident.

"Yeah, I'm sure," I answered. "You know I didn't kidnap her, right?"

"Yeah, I know," he admitted, still eyeing me suspiciously. "And I know that dead man on the elevator over in Uptown was self defense. She told me last night. Otherwise I might not be helping you out right about now." I declined to tell him about Loup Garou, not wanting his code to protect and serve to be blemished any further by the games people play.

"You want a ride? I can't take you far, but—"

"Nah, I'll walk. The fresh air will do me some good," I said, hobbling along behind him as I gingerly touched the war wounds covering most of my torso.

"This is it?"

"Yup," I said, shaking his hand as we came to a clearing where he'd left his police cruiser.

"If I see you again . . ."

"I know. You'll have to do your job. I understand. Now go on. Get outta here."

I'd approached and met with Officer Kane a few weeks earlier, after finding out which members of Dallas PD were assigned to Collette. He was one of the rare ones to volunteer. Then when I saw his face, I recognized him from the fake break-in at her place. He was the one who chose to stay behind to write the report while the others left. An emotional attachment, he had. An attachment I exploited to hatch this scheme.

Simple.

Collette would get what she needed to move on with her life.

If it were as I feared, I figured she wasn't a good enough shot to aim for my head. I wore the red jacket, thinking that if she really did pull the trigger, it would give her a nice bright target in the dark, especially if her vision wasn't back to one hundred percent. It was a major risk using real bullets, but Officer Kane knew what he was doing. He'd come through where she'd failed.

And in the end, he'd get the girl. That is, if his heart was true and his game was tight. The sum I'd deposited into an offshore account in his name would make for a nice honeymoon gift one day, if I saw the future correctly for them.

Who knows? Maybe I could try my hand at manipulation as cupid for them; to create, rather than destroy.

Appreciating the irony, I chuckled to myself before the rib pain almost brought me to tears.

For Truth was stranger than fiction.

Epilogue

Monaco

1 year later

"Welcome back, Monsieur Spielberg," the valet said, opening the door to my restored MGB Roadster as I returned to Hôtel de Paris from a day on the town.

"Don't scratch it," I said curtly as I exited, barely acknowledging his presence. I didn't have to, for the gambling profile of Elvis Spielberg didn't just register in Vegas; it spanned the ocean, garnering attention even in the midst of a spectacle such as the Global Music Awards taking place this weekend.

I'd spent the past year jaunting about Europe, blowing more money than I won, but establishing myself nonetheless ahead of my arrival in Monaco last week. I carried myself like the high roller I pretended to be as I jogged up the stairs under the canopy. The uniformed doorman smiled, throwing the doors to the palatial hotel open for me, granting me entry into the majestic ornate lobby built in 1864.

Beyond the standard high-end elite, I was met by an international who's who of entertainment—Shakira, Paul McCartney, Björk, Kylie Minogue and Shahrukh Khan, to name the ones I recognized immediately. Most were either returning from a day of yachting and photo ops or heading out in anticipation of a night of partying prior to tomorrow's awards show. I quietly slid among them, not interested in the festivities or the paparazzi outside along Place du Casino.

One party tonight held particular significance for a guest of the hotel. My contact inside his camp had kept me up to speed on it all. It was to be a celebration of his accomplishments. Almost a coronation, if you will.

But what is it they say about the best-laid plans?

As I entered the elevator to the Suite Garnier, I reflected on how successful my contact had been in getting so close to him. She'd been in my target's camp for the past six months, having "accidentally" run into him in Las Vegas, the place where he'd first met her—and he had wanted her ever since.

Of course, I knew that at the time.

"Are you with the music people?" the elevator operator dared ask in his best English, his disdain briefly showing.

"No. I actually have a life. No time for dealing with fantasies and ridiculousness," I answered in his native French, startling him. Once that was overcome, he acknowledged his pleasure in my answer.

"That one on this floor," he said in French as the elevator stopped. "One of those American bigshots. He's supposed to receive an award from the Prince tonight."

"Well, good for him," I said. "Maybe he'll be on his way then."

At the door to the suite where "that one" was staying, I passed by, instead entering the adjacent suite with my key. Once inside, I quickly walked over to the connecting door, opened mine then knocked once. His entourage would still be on the yacht at the suggestion of my contact, having wanted some one-on-one time with him before he was to receive the Principality's award for music executive of the year.

As I was about to knock a second time, my contact answered.

"You don't have much time," she said, wearing nothing more than a smile and a mischievous wink. As she clung to her gathered clothes in one hand, I could smell him on her nude body. She loved it—the danger and the thrill of the moment. In a sense, she was the perfect person for this.

A lot like me, you might say.

I entered his suite, the more opulent one, scoping the nineteenth century decor of the large entrance hall. Definitely suitable for royalty, or at least the modern day equivalent. Through the windows at the far end of the suite, I could see the full-length terrace overlooking the Place du Casino. Avoiding the possibility of anyone seeing me from outside, I cautiously walked the length of the spacious grand suite, checking the other rooms for anything unforeseen, and making sure there would be no witnesses.

Jason North was in his bedroom, standing solely in pair of boxers. I was given the rare glimpse of the blubbery girth surrounding his mid-section, it having expanded along with his wealth and power over the years. He jiggled a pair of cufflinks in one hand and a glass of wine in the other as he surveyed the tuxedo lying across the bed he'd just shared with the beautiful woman.

"Tiffany! Is my shower ready?" he yelled.

Good memory on her. She'd used the same name from their first meeting that time long ago. Made the gradual seduction more believable, easier to work over the coming months, with me feeding her what to say all along. He hummed something to himself while stroking his goatee, a quiet moment of self-admiration apparent.

"Big night?" I asked, causing him to drop his wine glass as he noticed me standing there in the mirror. Rather than breaking, the glass simply rolled around, relinquishing its contents onto the expensive carpet. Jason almost stepped on it himself.

"Truth," he voiced as he turned around to face me. "Christ, you scared me."

"Hello, Jason. Miss me?" I said, smiling over the fact that I'd rattled him.

"Of course, dear boy," he answered while reaching for more clothing to put on. In his gush of sudden modesty, he again almost stepped on the glass. "No one's heard from you in like forever. We thought you were—"

"Dead. You thought I was dead," I said, giving voice to his dark thoughts.

Of course he did.

I had Officer Kane take a picture of me back in Texas as I lay there shot up. Then I had him anonymously e-mail it to Lorelei Smart with

4Shizzle. A little gift left out there for any parties that might be interested in my wellbeing. I'm sure it choked Jason up to learn his dear nephew had met an unfortunate end.

Yet, here I was.

Alive, despite his attempts at betraying me to Collette and selling me out to Penny Antnee.

"Where's Tiffany?"

"Busy," I said with a chuckle as he hastily put on a pair of pants. "Look at you, the world at your feet. All your scheming, blackmailing, and backstabbing finally paying off," I said, applauding him mockingly as I took a few steps toward him. "Bravo. You're a Titan. A figure of myth."

"I'm not understanding you, Truth," he said, feigning defiance while retreating an equal number of steps. "I hate it when you ramble like your mother."

"Like mother like son, I suppose. Or maybe more like father, like son."

"Excuse me?" Jason said, exhibiting a faint nervous laugh. "I don't even know who your father is. And I doubt your mother did either."

"I think you do," I stated, picking up his Black-Berry from the antique chest of drawers beside me. He noticed the latex gloves I wore. I watched his throat rise with a gulp. "See, that's where the mythology lesson comes in. You really are like one of those Greek gods, ruling from on high, sticking your nose in the affairs of mere mortals as you see fit."

"Like you're any better," he huffed. I watched his hands as he clenched and flexed them, cuff-links still being held. Maybe he'd use them as weapons and hurl them at me.

"Never said I was. Ever heard of Cronus? See, he was a Titan who killed his father, Uranus. Then he became ruler, and took his sister, Rhea, as his wife. Crazy stuff, huh?"

"Crazy. Good term, because you are as crazy as your mother, I see," he prodded.

"Problem was that things have a history of repeating themselves. There came a time when Cronus had a child—a son, Zeus—and a time when the son returned to strike down the father once again. Just a wild, vicious cycle."

"I hate seeing you like this. Perhaps I can get some help for you, nephew."

"You know what I've noticed? You only call me nephew when you need self-assurance. You can drop the act. I know you're my father."

Jason stroked his goatee, but it was false this time. No confidence to it. A rehearsed motion with no substance or heart behind it. My mother was clearly the better actor of the two. Rather than speak, he just shook his head in the negative.

"Is that how she lost her mind? What was it? Did you rape her? Did you want her to have an abortion? Is that why she ran away and had me in New Mexico?"

"Stop, Truth."

"Uh-huh. My name had a greater meaning than the town where I was born, but it took till now to realize it," I said as it dawned on me. "It was that I was the truth staring you in the face when my mom returned to New Orleans. That's why she slapped the fuck out of you when you dared to play ignorant when we first met. Your denial of me as your son and what you did—that was the lie."

"You don't know what you're talking about. Now give me my fucking phone and get out of here!"

I ignored him, continuing. "The great Jason North in an incestuous relationship that produced a bastard offspring, of all things. Then he politely prods his own sister off a bridge one day to ensure no one ever finds out. More scandal than even you could take, I imagine."

"Shut up! Shut up! That isn't true!" he barked as he stepped toward me.

"What are you gonna do, Jason? Kill me like you did Melvin way back? Kill me like you did my mom the day you did that to her? Is that how it goes?"

"Fuck you. I didn't kill Leila. And . . . and I sure as hell didn't sleep with her."

"In case you didn't know it, you don't lie well without preparation. Good-bye, Jason. Can't say that you'll be missed."

With the finality of my words setting in, he charged me, either to get to his phone or to try to overpower me. When he did, he finally stepped on that wine glass. It cracked beneath his weight.

"Arrrrh!" he hollered as a shard cut through his bare foot. And as he did that, I struck.

Swiftly. Smoothly.

A simple syringe filled with sixty milliliters of air that I'd held in my pocket until now.

I covered Jason's mouth, injecting the small gauge insulin needle right into his jugular as he pivoted away in pain from the cut.

I cradled his head to my chest as he winced. Rather than letting Jason plummet to the floor, I held him up, beating away his frantic hands as he descended from Mount Olympus where he dwelled.

"You should've left me alone. You really should have left me alone," I whispered as I hushed his frantic yelps. I closed my eyes, continuing to hold him.

Then he stopped. The air bubble had worked its way to his heart. No more spasms. No more fighting. Cardiac arrest.

Simply no more.

There was a knock at the front door to Jason's suite. Somebody back from the yacht. She'd warned me to hurry up.

Rather than panicking, I checked Jason a final time. Looked into his empty eyes and saw all the dark evil deeds we'd done together: all the black-mail jobs, all the intimidation tactics, my dispos-ing of Melvin for him during those pre-Katrina days. We really were like father and son.

I walked to the door, opening it before the knocking got out of hand. But it wasn't my con-tact.

A large, muscled, stoic figure greeted me.

I faced Penny Antnee, neither one of us choos-ing to speak at first.

"He gone?" he finally asked.

"Yeah," I replied. "Enjoy your empire. It's all yours."

"Good."

Until everything fell apart, I was only conduct-ing business. I'd leave it up to Penny to decide whether or not to come out of the closet, for at the end of the day, it was really none of my busi-ness.

We all have secrets that we live . . . and die with.

"You know we ain't straight over Loup," he said, deciding to admit the elephant in the room really existed. "That was my boy to the end."

"He tried to kill me. We'll never be straight over that," I said, looking him in the eye without blinking. "But are we okay?"

"Yeah. We okay," he begrudgingly acknowledged. In some illogical, random, circuitous way, we were even now. A war had been waged that we'd never speak of again.

"Final request of you," I said.

"What?" Penny asked, eager to enter the suite to see my handiwork.

"Push him off the terrace for me. Let him fall onto the street."

"Why?"

"It has some meaning for me," I replied, thoughts of my mother on the Mississippi River Bridge raw on my mind. I'd always suspected Jason's involvement; however, his reaction proved it. "He started having a heart attack, stumbled. Broke the glass in the bedroom with his foot. Staggered out to the terrace for some air or to try to call someone . . . and bam. Right over the ledge. Make sure to drag his bloody foot across the floor as if he walked on his own. Drop his BlackBerry over with him too. I played it in my head just now. It'll fly. The Prince hates scandals in his country."

Who knows? Perhaps I had something on the Prince. But that wasn't for Penny to know or consider.

"You's a sick motherfucker, man," he said with renewed swagger, resuming his gum chewing.

"One other thing."

"Damn, dude! Ain't you got somewhere to be? I wanna get up outta here."

"Natalia. Tell her I'm sorry about the blackmail job."

"Oh. We don't talk much since I signed with North, but I can do that," he said, switching to meekness. "It's going to be better now . . . for both of us." With that, he adjusted his fitted Miami Hurricanes baseball cap—odd combination with the Mediterranean linen he sported—and shuffled off to attend to North.

Downstairs, I slipped through the lobby once again, shrugging off pangs of melancholy as I exited through the front doors.

Free.

My antique Roadster spun around to pick me up, barely missing my foot. Its dreadful operator, unaccustomed to its right-sided steering wheel, was my contact inside Jason's camp.

Sophia.

Hey, someone with her skills was too valuable, no matter how enraged I was at the time.

I unloaded my gun into the floor that fateful day of reckoning back in California, missing her entirely, as I decided to be merciful for some reason and spare her life. In some twisted way, it turned her on.

A loud gasp erupted from the passing crowd as Jason's body plummeted from the other end of the building. It landed with a sick thud on the cobblestones, causing screams to ring out once the paparazzi realized it wasn't some music week prank. That was followed by a super nova of flashbulbs, replacing whatever must-have shot was important moments earlier. The valet attendants and door guards scrambled toward Jason's body, trying to maintain order and gain control of the situation. I didn't bother looking up, for no one would be in the window by now. Penny wasn't stupid.

All that would be left was the writing of obituaries and tributes to a man who changed the industry, yet deserved none of it.

"Where to, guvnah?" Sophia asked in a shaky cockney accent that seemed to amuse only her. It wasn't like we were in London.

This week.

"Wherever you want to go. It's a new day. Let's just enjoy it," I said as I jumped in the passenger seat.

With that simple instruction, my apprentice sped me away, down the coast and into obscurity.

Or maybe in search of more mayhem . . . if we chose.

We were myths, after all.

About the Author

Eric Pete is an *Essence* bestselling novelist. His works include: *Someone's In the Kitchen, Gets No Love, Don't Get It Twisted, Lady Sings the Cruels, Blow Your Mind, Sticks and Stones,* and *Reality Check*. He has also contributed to the anthologies *After Hours, Twilight Moods, and On the Line.* He currently resides in Texas where he is working on his next novel. His website is www.ericpete.com.

ORDER FORM
URBAN BOOKS, LLC
78 E. Industry Ct
Deer Park, NY 11729

Name: (please print):_____

Address:_____

City/State:_____

Zip:_____

QTY	TITLES	PRICE

Shipping and handling-add $3.50 for 1st book, then $1.75 for each additional book.

Please send a check payable to:

Urban Books, LLC

Please allow 4-6 weeks for delivery